Vizard

An Ember Files Side Story

Shari Marshall

Writing Sparkle Books
sharimarshall.ca
Alberta, Canada

Marshall, Shari
Vizard: An Ember Files Side Story

eBook ISBN 978-1-7782531-5-7
Paperback ISBN 978-1-7782531-4-0

Fiction | Fantasy | Urban
Fiction | Fantasy | Dark
Fiction | Fantasy | Contemporary

Praise for Vizard

"Fantastical creatures and vivid villains highlight this emotional tale that balances thrills, twists, and Rye's gutsy planning with intricate, imaginative worldbuilding and a crush of appealingly eccentric characters. Perfect for fans of inventive, character-driven fantasy, *Vizard* offers crisp yet evocative prose, brisk and funny dialogue, and a hero readers can't help but root for." — *BookLife*

"Marshall balances tragedy with lively descriptions of the magic system and unexpected moments of romance and drama . . . With her expert, evocative writing, Marshall breathes life into the fantasy world and its inhabitants, presenting them in a compelling and multi-dimensional manner while exploring themes of family, love, friendship, grief, revenge, identity, duty, and responsibility." — *BookView Review*

"With its intriguing and magical elements, the fantasy novella *Vizard* expands the world of the Ember Files series." — *Foreward* Clarion Review

"Fast-moving and fun for sorcery-loving YA fans, this quick read bounces from prison break-ins and romantic dabbles to fairy magic and soul-smashing battles, woven neatly with focused and animated storytelling." —*SPR*, starred review

Dedication

To you, the reader. Thank you for your belief in magic.

For me and all the faces I've worn.

For my parents: Stewart, Shirley, and Joseph.

Vizard

Chapter 1
Juniper Berry

A scream tears through the house with a force that rattles the windows. Ensley's eyes spring wide and she hits the stairs with Aaron on her heels. Their little Juniper Berry is the only other Spellbinder in the house, but for her to give such a piercing cry suggests they may no longer be alone. Neither Ensley nor Aaron gives any conscious thought to the orbs that form in their hands as they pound up the stairs toward their daughter. The silence that follows Juniper Berry's scream is heavy and foreboding.

Ensley drops into a sliding motion as she enters Juniper Berry's room, hoping to avoid any attack that might blitz the first person through the door. Sliding will draw attention down and away from the doorway to allow Aaron entry without immediate threat. Scanning, Ensley only sees her thirteen-year-old daughter standing with her eyes squeezed shut. Juniper Berry's hands are pressed so tight over her ears that she looks like she's trying to pop her own head like a balloon. Juniper Berry is frozen there. Alone.

Ensley is at Juniper Berry's side in seconds, orbs gone. She's cautious as she puts her hands over Juniper Berry's wrists and pushes down gently. Juniper Berry resists with surprising strength. Ensley locks her stare with Aaron, who gives a subtle head shake to show that there's no threat present. He releases his orbs. Ensley refocuses on her daughter. Something has terrified Juniper Berry, but her room is calm, marked by the rhythmic ticking of the clock and the organic chemical scent of markers and craft paper.

Ensley moves her hands to Juniper Berry's shoulder. She interlaces threads of magic, creating a soft weave of soothing air and brushes Juniper Berry's skin with it. Juniper Berry shudders, but a bit of the tension drains from her muscles. Ensley continues directing the air at her daughter. After a few shallow breaths, Juniper Berry takes a deep inhale and Ensley lowers Juniper Berry's hands from her ears.

"Shh, little Berry. Mom is here."

Juniper Berry opens and fixes her pale brown gaze on her mother's face. The terror shifts to pain, and Juniper Berry's body shakes with the sobs that follow.

"Juniper Berry?" Aaron says, crouching. She launches herself into her father's open arms. He holds her while she cries. He searches Ensley's face but finds his confusion mirrored there.

After a few minutes, Juniper Berry pushes out of her father's embrace. She swipes at the warm streaks on her cheeks that are cooling as they dry. The slight taste of salt is present on her tongue, snot and tears having crept into the corners of her mouth with her breaths. Ensley reaches out and takes hold of Juniper Berry's ponytail, stroking the three braids she wears there. "Okay, little Berry, what happened?"

Juniper Berry sniffles, but she straightens her spine. She speaks slowly. "I don't know. My room disappeared and I could see the front door of our house." She pauses and swallows. Her next words tumble out. "It exploded open, and three people came in. I couldn't see their faces because they were all wearing hoods, but . . ."

Her lip trembles. She crosses her arms, angry at her quivering. She hefts her chin up a bit. "They killed us." Despite her tough bravado, tears leak from the corner of her eyes.

Ensley pulls Juniper Berry into a hug and holds her tight, still stroking her silky braids. "Vision?" she whispers to Aaron over Juniper Berry's head.

Aaron considers and shakes his head when he can't come up with any other option. Not wanting to overwhelm Juniper Berry, Aaron keeps his expression neutral as he magically projects his voice into Ensley's ear so Juniper Berry can't hear. "It fits with her other abilities, like her power of observation and ability to read people. And think about how she learns so quickly, simply by watching." He raises an eyebrow. "How much time do you think we have?"

Ensley shrugs. Loosening her grip on Juniper Berry, Ensley moves her daughter out to arm's length. She keeps her hands on Juniper Berry's shoulders so the soft flow of magic can continue working its calming effects. "Juniper Berry, Dad and I believe you've had your first vision. We'll explain more about it later, but first, can you tell us if you noticed anything else with what you saw?" Ensley smiles at her daughter, proud of her developing powers.

Juniper Berry scrunches her face up. Aaron stands. On edge with Juniper Berry's premonition, he magically amplifies his hearing. They aren't expecting company, so any unexpected visitors need to be considered a potential threat. His decision gives them a split second of warning that the nightmare is about to enact itself. He kisses Juniper Berry on the top of her head, drawing in a whiff of the honeyed, floral, and woodsy fragrance of her hair, and whispers his love. He turns to Ensley. "I'll buy you time to hide her." With a fast kiss on her lips, he races from the room with sparks of magic flaring on his fingertips.

Ensley locks eyes with Juniper Berry and sees her daughter's fear. With a smile Ensley pulls her in for another hug, using the time to school her own features. "I'm so proud of you, Rye." The use of Juniper Berry's birth name, Rye, is the one crack in Ensley's composed façade. "Always remember how proud your father and I are of you, my little Juniper Berry."

"Mom?" Juniper Berry's voice is infused with the calmness of the magic Ensley suffused her with.

Ensley kisses her daughter's pale cheek. "Come now, I need you to go into the hidey."

The house's air currents vibrate with a violent expansion of energy and a thundering bang as the front door explodes. Ensley scoops Juniper Berry up, thankful for her small stature. Juniper Berry's thirteen years of age appear on her as if she's ten. Ensley rushes her words as she stows Juniper Berry away. "Remember not to come through the house, Juniper Berry. There will be things there you won't want to see." She kisses her on the forehead. "I love you." Ensley seals her daughter into the secret hiding space and races toward the battle.

Ensley can't see the intruders when she crests the top of the staircase, but she's in time to see a death orb slam into Aaron at the bottom of the stairs. It happens in slow motion. Electricity throbs inside death orbs, a frenzied pulse. An orb so purple that it's almost black convulses with crackles of lime green inside as it flows through the air, unnoticed, on Aaron's right. He's protecting himself from another death orb, rich black with agitated pops of violet and green, thrown from the left. He doesn't make a noise when it hits him. His body explodes, leaving a sparkling mist clinging to the air. Ensley screams, unaware that the sound is coming from her.

Her eyebrows lower, her nostrils flare, and her lips tighten. Her lungs are searing from the odour of burnt wire, a sweet pungent smell, in the wake of the attack on Aaron. Ensley hasn't used a death orb or even considered forming one before, but the weave comes to her unbidden. A survival instinct in response to the anger, fear, and anguish that strikes her at that moment.

Her sudden appearance and quick response benefit her. As two intruders step into sight at the bottom of the stairs, Ensley throws her orbs. They're cherry-coloured orbs pulsing with a deep wine shade. They slam into two of the intruders. Ensley doesn't see the misty particles of their bodies leave a dusty substance on the floor because a rope of magic catches her feet, yanking them out from under her. The last intruder jerks the rope violently, pulling Ensley down the stairs. The back of her head bashes off every step on the way down. She isn't conscious when she hits the bottom.

The hooded attacker stands over her, unsatisfied that her death was swift. He pushes his hood off as if it hinders his view of her lifeless body. The corners of his mouth twitch, approaching a smile, as he violates Ensley's body with a volt of magic that arches her off the floor and slams her down for the last time.

With a contented sigh, he reaches out with feelers of magic, searching for the child, the third to be killed. He searches not once but twice, sensing no other presence in the house. His eyes squint and dart from side to side. He waits, listening, just standing rooted to the spot. He's confident that a child can't outwait him. If the child is in the house hiding, somehow avoiding detection from his magic, his patience and soundlessness will be its undoing.

Hours pass in silence before he pulls up his hood, steps into the shadows, and vanishes into the deepening night.

Chapter 2
Juniper Berry

Juniper Berry wakes to silence. The world around her is dark. Startled, she sits up fast. Her head cracks off something above her. She feels with her hands, finding the clingy, sticky threads of spiderwebs coating the coffin-like walls. She stretches her toes down to find a wall there too. Her nose detects the musty evidence of old wood and freshly disturbed dust.

Her foggy brain works to fight the panic. She closes her eyes, drawing deliberate breaths the way her mother taught her to. Juniper Berry's memory jolts as if she's hearing the softness of her mother's voice at that very moment. She glimpses her mother's face, with brown eyes and soft wrinkle lines in the corners, peering into her own as sparkling particles drift over her, tickling her skin. Through the sparkling particles, Juniper Berry sees love foremost in her mother's expression.

Her mother put her in the hidey. *Hidey* is what Juniper Berry's parents call this secret space, a crawl space between the interior and exterior walls of the house. The angle of the roof creates a low slanted ceiling in this section of the upstairs, which allowed for the inside wall to be framed with a small pocket of undetectable space behind it. As she lies in the hidey, everything floods back into her memory. The particles were a sleep charm—eternal sleep—one so strong that it slowed Juniper Berry's heart rate to a point somewhere on the brink of death. It's a dangerous charm. Few Spellbinders can enact the charm without killing the subject; eternal sleep hasn't been actively taught in hundreds of years.

The cruelty associated with eternal sleep encouraged Spellbinders to make it an obsolete teaching. Why or how Ensley mastered the charm, Juniper Berry doesn't know, and she never thought to ask. Her mother placed her under eternal sleep once before so that Juniper Berry would know what it was and how it felt. It seemed like a strange practice, but Juniper Berry saw no need to question her mother about it.

Her mother is a strong Spellbinder with secrets to teach, secrets that die—

Her mother put her to sleep, hid her, and . . .

Juniper Berry, eyes still closed, allows her grief to wash over her. Both her parents are gone, murdered.

She wouldn't be hiding in a crawl space under magical wards if they were alive. The weight of her grief overwhelms Juniper Berry, who cries until sleep overcomes her.

It's impossible to tell how much time has passed, but Juniper Berry can't stay hidden forever. She shifts onto her stomach and pushes at the wall above her head, mumbling the secret words she knows will allow her to override the wards. "Were you guys afraid of something?" she whispers to her lamented parents. "Is that why you made me learn to control the magic in the hidey?"

The door gives way, soundless. The room outside the crawl space is lit by pre-morning light. Juniper Berry pushes out with a tiny feeler of magic to ensure nobody is lingering in the house. Satisfied, she drags herself out. She runs down the hall past the stairs without looking toward them. Her mother's warning is fresh in her mind. Juniper Berry slows when she enters her own bedroom, scanning, lost about what to do next. Although her parents taught her how to use the magic of the hidey, none of them expected Juniper Berry to emerge alone. One parent or both should be here.

Juniper Berry's mouth feels dry as she shoves a few items of clothing into a backpack. Her hands tremble with the zipper. She tries to ignore the dull ache inside herself.

There's a creak on the floorboards downstairs. Her blood freezes in her veins. She holds her breath, straining to hear over the thundering of her heartbeat. Her feelers didn't detect life forms, but maybe there's something less detectable waiting for her. She doesn't want to find out.

Juniper Berry casts about for something special to take with her. Maybe she can sneak into her parent's bedroom to find something there. Her desperation is at war with her panic. Another creak. *No time.*

She steels herself, promising she won't cry. Easing the window up, she slides her backpack over her shoulders and clambers out onto the small piece of roof that angles toward the old triangular television antenna, intending to climb down its ladder-like tower. The air is fresh and a few stars still have a glowing presence in the sky. The sight of them acts like a trigger for her, a reminder that she's alone and fleeing from her home instead of being snug in her bed with her parents asleep down the hall. "You're not focusing, Little Berry," she tells herself in her best Mother impression.

Juniper Berry directs her attention inside herself, locking onto the unique patch of blue that feels like a song. She recognizes the familiar force exerting itself on her entire body, and the world transforms. Juniper Berry opens her wings and takes flight. She can see her bird's body, unique to her, unique because female indigo bunting birds are brown, but she's a beautiful blue. An anomaly if she were a true bird species, but because she's a shapeshifter, her bird's traits are altered, making her unique.

She takes a low flight around the house, heedless of the danger that may be waiting. There's a pain inside her she can't describe, and the thought of flying away from her childhood home, alone, with no kind of goodbye, is crushing. Her breathing is becoming erratic as her emotions threaten to consume her. That's all it takes, and she loses hold of her bird form and hits the ground with a thud.

She has no time to catch her breath or calm her emotions. Bolting upright, she's not sure if the impact of her hitting the ground has alerted anyone inside the house to her presence. She still isn't sure if there is someone in the house. She resettles her backpack into a comfortable position. Another distinctive quality of shapeshifting is the shifter's ability to transform their clothing and items associated with their person in and out of bird form.

Juniper Berry notes that she's in the grass behind her house. By the back door, there's a strange red symbol. The red reminds her of her mother's wine. Juniper Berry tips her head to the side. The symbol is two flames, abstract-shaped hands, holding and releasing swirling wind. Terror creeps over her, its millions of centipede legs tickling their way up her spine.

Juniper Berry pulls her eyes from the symbol. She knows it's meant for Spellbinders to see, a warning, just like she knows when the normie police show up, they won't see it. If there are bodies inside, they'll see those, but they won't see anything magic. They can't. They're conditioned not to see it. The magical things they do experience, they reason away as science, coincidence, superstition, anything but what it is. Juniper Berry casts a hurried look at her surroundings. With the unknown image burned into her mind, she locks onto that inner piece of herself and transforms, determined to not let anything break her focus. She plays over the first part of her mother's instructions in her mind as she pumps her wings, propelling herself higher and farther from her home. *Go to Allurist Detention Centre.*

Juniper Berry's wings are tired, and she's only made it the few miles to the next neighbour's home. She feels like a target so high in the sky, so she dives toward the beautiful yellow field of flowers on the opposite side of the closest house. Flapping her wings a few more times before shifting, she thinks of her mother. Juniper Berry likes shifting from bird to human form a bit off the ground to feel herself fall and land on her feet, but she also did it to tease her mother. The first time Juniper Berry did it she misjudged her height and she fell, spraining her ankle and scaring Ensley. They made a joke about it later, and both of them would make surprised faces when Juniper Berry would transform in the air. Making her surprise face in memory of her mother, Juniper Berry drops into the canola with her jaw agape. She gets a mouth full of the yellow plant. It feels peculiar and causes her to spit and push her tongue against her teeth until her tongue flops out of her mouth, grinding away the saliva-covered squashed petals.

She walks for miles without being seen. Her shoulders slump forward, and her chin hangs down, the weight of her situation bearing down on her. Juniper Berry's tummy grumbles in response to the food-like smell of the canola plant. She keeps walking but adjusts her backpack so she can dig inside it. Smiling, she pulls out a cereal bar and thanks herself for always hiding snacks in her bag. Walking and chewing are mechanical, but the bar is dry, like gravelly sand grating between her teeth. Regardless, the rhythm of the two actions lulls her mind. She imagines herself lost in a yellow forest, searching for faeries.

The repeating yelp of a police siren jars her from her daydreams. It doesn't take long for the din of rubber speeding over the pavement to pass by. She picks up her pace, desperate to put more distance between herself and . . . and what? She doesn't know what to call this.

There isn't time to let hopelessness overtake her. She lifts her chin, pulls her shoulders back, and pushes and transforms, flying low over the canola until the sun fades from the sky. Juniper Berry soars into the loft of a barn and shifts. Her tired body doesn't dwell on the pokes from the hay as she falls asleep.

Chapter 3
Juniper Berry

Commotion below the barn loft startles Juniper Berry from her sleep. Her muscles clench as she listens, assessing for threats. It's just a morning routine going on in the barn. Early, the sky through the open window is still hazy with night. She lies still, waiting, enjoying the sweet woody smell of the hay.

I need a plan. I can't fly and walk from Alberta to British Columbia and then deep into the Yukon. With a sigh, she decides she needs transportation. She lies there, wondering if she can steal a vehicle from this farm.

As the farmer and his wife walk out of the barn, Juniper Berry strains to hear the conversation. The wife's voice is muffled with sadness. "We gotta make the drive tomorrow if we're going to be there for the funeral, Henry." Smacking her hand over her mouth to stifle a laugh at her luck, Juniper Berry doesn't hear what else is said because the wife's sniffles and the crunch of gravel overpower the conversation.

Henry, the farmer, is driving to the Yukon tomorrow morning, probably not as far as Juniper Berry needs to go, but to the Yukon. Her happiness at her luck merges with guilt because of the reason for the farmer's travels; a death in the family. *Family, I don't have one anymore!* Her vision blurs, and her eyelids feel hot from their battle against her unshed tears. She waits till there's silence before shifting and flying off in search of food and water.

She spends the day in the fields around the farm. Juniper Berry wants to know a little more about this farmer and his wife before stowing away in their vehicle. Periodically, over the day, she flies in and lands where she can watch one or the other of them completing their chores. They work hard, breaking to eat lunch together and talking kindly to one another.

More than once, Juniper Berry imagines her mother's voice telling her to trust her abilities. "You know that prickling sense when something feels wrong, that instinct that keeps us safe? That response to unseen stimuli?" she would ask. "Well, you have that. But when you focus, you can read so much more about a person than the rest of us. You know with certainty what's there and how to respond. Trust what you read in those moments, Juniper Berry. It'll never steer you wrong."

Juniper Berry knows her mother is correct. And even though it's a talent she's still trying to understand, her ability allows her to read the balance of good and evil within people. With that in mind, coupled with what she's learned of Henry and his wife, she decides she'll be safe travelling with this farm couple.

Once the farm falls into silence, she returns to the loft to sleep. The moonlight illuminates the particles of dust and chaff in the air as she rustles the hay, and the floorboards creak as she finds a comfy spot. She sleeps solidly and almost misses her free ride in the morning.

As the truck crunches slowly down the gravel driveway, Juniper Berry transforms and flies after it. She swoops down onto the back bumper and waits a few minutes. The truck rumbles to a stop before turning out into traffic. Juniper Berry uses the opportunity to shift, needing her hands to maneuver the tarp and slip under it into the truck. She's grateful the tarp is breathable, or the faint rotten egg odour from the box of this farm truck would be overpowering.

The farmer sets a steady driving pace, stopping late several nights for brief roadside sleeping. July turns to August as they travel the isolated roads. Juniper Berry peeks at the passing scenery from time to time, noting that it's trees and no houses, no shops, and no gas stations. Bears lumber along the side of the road. There are elk, deer, and moose. On occasion, bison block the road completely. She takes it all in with wide eyes, thankful for the distractions.

Juniper Berry loses track of time after having stowed away in the truck. It's early morning on what she thinks is their third day of travel when she slips from the box. She knows they're deep in the Yukon, and she has just a short distance left to travel. The air is crisp and tastes cleaner than the air she has breathed before. She doesn't question it. Instead, Juniper Berry pulls in deep breaths and with no magic required she cleanses herself with them. She transforms and takes flight.

By the time she reaches the base of the mountain where Allurist Detention Centre is located, the day is gray with mist so thick Juniper Berry can't see more than a few feet in front of her. The sun is a hazy ball in the sky, obscured by the heavy fog. There's a dampness in the air that coats her skin with minuscule beads of moisture. She knows as this day wears on it's going to deepen into a cold with the possibility of snow, as preposterous as snow is in August. Her Canadian northern climate project demonstrates its worth as she recalls what it taught her about the weather. Juniper Berry's so far north that the weather isn't what she's accustomed to. She risks freezing to death if she doesn't reach and gain access to Allurist Detention Centre.

Deciding on a combination of climbing and flying, she starts up the mountain. The wind whistles along the slopes. Pebbles displace and slide as she climbs. Juniper Berry realizes her actions are getting more challenging due to exhaustion and the change in air pressure. She stifles a yawn and tries to ignore her icy fingers, hoping that her feathery form will offer her a bit of warmth for the next segment of her flight.

She hasn't gone far when the mountain reveals a ledge that wasn't visible before. Juniper Berry understands that it wasn't noticeable from the lower elevation. In addition, the ledge is a large area of land disguised using magic. Allurist Detention Centre looms, built right into the face of the mountain. Thoughts of the Spellbinder prison are daunting, seeing it is intimidating. Casting around for a place to land and hide, Juniper Berry notes trees don't grow at this altitude. She settles for the cold ground behind a mound of stone and rubble.

Juniper Berry sits blinking at the building, her mind grappling to put the words *castle* and *prison* into one description. The stone of the building is weather-beaten and aged, yet beautiful. The section of the structure that faces the mountain ledge is wider than the front of a modern house, but it rises thirty feet with tiny, recessed windows. Two walls angle off the main section and sink into the rough mountain surface. The only visible entrance to Allurist Detention Centre is an open archway that falls into shadows so deep that what lies beyond them isn't visible from Juniper Berry's vantage point.

This isn't a place I can just walk in and out of. So, now what do I do? She pushes away the tickle of dread rolling in her stomach. Everything depends on this part of her mother's instructions to obtain a specific envelop. Juniper Berry can't turn away.

Watching is getting her nowhere. Nobody has come

in or out, and Juniper Berry's body has a heaviness that doesn't fit physical exhaustion. Before she can overthink her decision, she shifts. Flying as close to the archway as possible, she lands in the shadows and re-assumes her regular-sized human form for a second. As she enacts her plan, she smiles and stifles a giggle at the feeling of the pit of her stomach lurching upwards and back again like her body was propelled over a hill in a fast-moving vehicle. Changing into a smaller-sized person always creates that belly feeling.

Stomach hill, her parents called it when they first taught her to shrink. For Juniper Berry, it was the greatest feeling in the world, a big belly tickle, with the reward of being the same four-inch-tall height as her parents. When else can a child be an equal height to an adult? With the thought of her parents, her smile fades. *I promised. No tears.*

The cold from the wall sinks into her as she pushes against it. At four inches tall, slinking in the dim light like a scared mouse will make getting closer to her goal easier. Juniper Berry's current time constraint is the cold. The archway is a deep tunnel that leads to a gated entrance; the door is open behind the gate. She's almost to it when the clatter of feet echoes in her small ears like a series of bombs moving toward her. Juniper Berry freezes with her hands pressed tight over her ears, working a magic weave to filter sounds.

The gate flies open forcefully. Juniper Berry is stunned by the appearance of the creature associated with the footfalls. Her mouth gaps open, and her breath is a gulp. The rush of freezing air into her lungs chokes her. Terror fills her as she tries to stifle a cough. The frumpy creature dresses in shades of brown, including a decrepit pair of work boots. Between the intentional stomping of its feet and the angry monologue, Juniper Berry's coughing goes unnoticed. There's no danger of the creature seeing her because a pointed brown hat obscures its vision.

Juniper Berry's mouth forms an open O. *Earth dweller!* She has heard stories of Earth dwellers but never imagined she would see one. Distracted, she magically amplifies her vision, noting first that the Earth dweller's nose is so bulbous it's keeping the hat from dropping to its neck. The visible skin of its face is fog-grey and unnaturally smooth.

"Of course, there are female gnomes. Spellbinder woodenhead! Do I not look like a woman? Is my name, Adva, not a female name?" The Earth dweller grumbles as she brings her hands to her baggy brown shirt and cups breasts that wouldn't have been visible otherwise. "Call me in, day after day, to draft the blueprints, decipher previous schematics, and ensure the prisoner wards are holding. Ungrateful tomfools—" She stops, jumps up, and pounds her three-foot-high, fifty-pound self down on one spot.

For the shrunken Juniper Berry, the earth moves like an earthquake, and she barely keeps her footing. A grating racket fills the air. The Earth dweller jumps up and forward, disappearing into a hole she opened when she pounded the ground. More grinding indicates the hole's closing. *Earth dwellers live in the mountains around the prison.*

Juniper Berry gives her head a shake to clear it. She notices that the moisture she expels when she breathes is crystalizing and heavy snow is falling. The gate has swung shut, which isn't a problem for her current size. The Earth dweller, in her angry rant, left the main door open. Juniper Berry considers magical wards but dismisses them because who would break into a prison? Of course, there are wards, but they're set up to keep prisoners from breaking out. It's unlikely a normie would ever find this Spellbinder prison, given its location and that it's magically hidden.

Juniper Berry squeezes through the bars and gets her first view of the interior of the Allurist Detention Centre.

Chapter 4
Juniper Berry

Juniper Berry is standing in a square-shaped, two-storey brick room illuminated by cylinder-shaped lights suspended from the second-floor ceiling. She takes in the space. The upper floor is visible through polished black bars, revealing hallways of brick and metal with dim lighting and no people. She can see cells. Every Spellbinder has a measure of respect mixed with fear and wonder when the jail cells of the Allurist Detention Centre are part of a conversation because each cell controls the magical strengths of the prisoner inside it. When out of their cells, each inmate is fitted with ankle cuffs that inhibit the use of magic, including the ability to shrink and shapeshift.

Straight ahead of Juniper Berry is a glass wall

framed out with the same black metal. On the other side of the glass, people are milling about. She remains unnoticed, but fear washes through her like a fire. She has come too far to get caught. Her legs move before the rest of her has figured out what she's doing. The main room has a closed, heavy steel door to the left, but the one on the right is open. Her mother told her the door will be open. How Ensley would know that, Juniper Berry doesn't know and she doesn't question it. The open door is her destination.

Juniper Berry dismisses the quiver of her body as her nerves. She also dismisses the slight prickling that stings her flesh, thinking it's nothing more than a ward she crossed through when she entered the room. The new room is empty and, by a stroke of luck, appears to be the office she needs. She dashes to the far side of the room and starts sifting through the desk.

Voices come out of nowhere.

Juniper Berry can see the owner of a squealing voice standing in profile in the doorway, looking toward the prisoners. He's short, wearing a crumpled pale grey suit. His peanut-shaped head has a five o'clock shadow. Before she can react, the man turns and enters. His partner's footsteps clack on the tile floor, moving away from them. The man's face, flat and indistinctive, scrunches up questioningly at the sight of Juniper Berry. She's curious why her being in his office isn't unexpected; he appears to have questions but is not surprised. Juniper Berry stares back at him, hoping her face is pure defiance.

"Adva, what are you still doing here? I thought you left to review the schematics in the comfort of," he sneers, "your stone hole."

Adva? Juniper Berry's mouth drops open, and she gapes at the man, processing what he said. It's just the man and Juniper Berry in the room. The man is addressing Juniper Berry as if he has mistaken her for Adva. Juniper Berry can't keep her hand from flying to her face or from flinching when it smacks the big, round nose attached there. She feels confused as her fingers trace the smoothest skin she has ever felt. It's not her skin or her nose, but it's on the face attached to her.

Her confusion deepens when her fingers brush against a hat nestled low on her head. *I look like the earth dweller,* her brain whispers. She glances down at herself to see a short, round frame clothed in oversized brown burlap. She snaps her mouth shut and pulls her eyes up fast to the man. Her quivering body and tingling skin weren't nerves and wards. She magically altered her appearance without conscious intention. She did it without knowing she even could.

"Needed this," her voice rumbles out. She lifts a pale blue scroll from the desk, infusing it with orbs, and whips it with as much force as she can toward the man. They both watch as it spins end over end through the air, shooting five tiny orbs out of the cylinder at the man's head. "Psychedelic," he squeals as each orb hits his forehead with a pop. He slumps to the floor, asleep. He'll experience a series of images and sensations for hours before he wakes, feeling disorientated and confused. He won't remember the orbs or anyone being in his office.

Juniper Berry doesn't have time to be pleased with her fast thinking. She races over and pulls the unconscious man out of the doorway. When she moves his body with ease, she's surprised by the strength this Earth dweller physic affords her. She dashes back to the desk and slams her meaty hand down. The bang bounces through the room, masking the soft clink the desk makes. If the one-inch-thick piece of wood hadn't bumped into Juniper Berry's body, she wouldn't have known that a secret drawer unlatched. She moves back a step, pulling the drawer open enough to reveal a surface that has a slight indent notched into the wood with a sealed pale brown envelope nestled in it.

She scoops it up, stuffs it into her baggy clothes, and slams the secret drawer. The sharp sound of heeled feet moving across the tile sends alarms through Juniper Berry. The man's female partner is returning, a guard or perhaps his secretary?

A stinging tingle ripples over her skin, and she fights the urge to scratch herself all over. It's the same feeling she felt when she was worried about being caught at the main entrance and she raced into this room. Juniper Berry acknowledges it isn't a ward causing the strange sensation on her body. She's accessing magic in herself that she didn't know she had, magic currently accessed and driven by self-preservation. It's unusual, but the things Juniper Berry has experienced since her parent's death—including their murder—is unorthodox. She's altered her appearance so that she no longer looks like Adva.

Hurrying past the unconscious man, she hastens out of the room. The bitter scent of coffee fills the foyer. Juniper Berry and the woman both stop walking. Silence falls around them as they look each other over. Juniper Berry holds her breath, waiting to see if her impersonation of the man will hold up. Neither of them speaks. The echo of the woman's heels moving away with her cup of coffee drowns Juniper Berry's sigh.

Juniper Berry breaks into a run, plowing through the door. She doesn't look back to find out if her abrupt departure drew any attention. The thumping of her feet gives way to the flapping of her wings as she flees from the Allurist Detention Centre.

At the edge of the mountain, Juniper Berry arcs her bird body up before she angles down into a plunging dive, another first. The freezing air speeding past her is thrilling. Everything about the last few hours has been exhilarating. She closes her eyes and lets herself free fall, pulling out of the dive when she senses the ground approaching.

Her initial plan of hiding and sleeping inside the Allurist Detention Centre is forgotten. Juniper Berry needs to find somewhere warm, fast. Frost clings to her feathers and her wings feel stiff. She pushes herself harder than she ever thought she could. When she reaches a subdued town, the only lights visible are from a late-night gas station.

A transport truck is parked at the pumps. They're as

far north as the road goes, so the transport must be returning to civilization. She swoops in close and shifts, stumbling on her frozen legs. She pulls the door open, climbs up and shrinks, but she's too cold to enjoy the feeling of stomach hill that accompanies her change in size. The cab is warm and has a savoury fragrance of smoke and spice. Ignoring the screaming of her limbs as the heat defrosts her, she hurries into the back part of the sleeper cab.

The floor is littered with discarded clothes. She grabs a shirt that doesn't stink and pulls it under the bed. Nestling into the shirt, she waits. She doesn't dare peek out when the truck door slams shut, and the truck springs to life. The swaying movement, coupled with the warmth and deep continuous groan of the engine, makes Juniper Berry aware of her tiredness. She isn't worried about being found. The driver has other clothes and things to focus on rather than what might be hiding under the bed. Before regular sleep overtakes her, she weaves a soft sleep charm over herself to enhance the length of her slumber. She wants to be as close as possible to the next leg of her journey when she wakes.

Within seconds, she is lulled to sleep.

Chapter 5
Juniper Berry

As she sleeps, she dreams. Images of herself flash through her mind. At least it feels like herself, but it isn't, because her appearance isn't the same. *Who am I?* The question lingers in her sleepy brain as she wakes to the truck door slamming shut. From the muffled voices outside, she hears someone say Calgary. *Calgary? How long did I sleep? Days?*

Juniper Berry has no time for a slow wake-up. She can hear the footsteps of the driver approaching the transport. She races through the cab in her shrunken size. The windows are open, so she shifts and flies out of the passenger side. The sun feels warm on her wings and it's so bright that it's almost blinding. She soars high and circles as she tries to get her bearings. The airport isn't hard to pick out with all the air traffic coming and going.

Her bladder is aching with need. She takes advantage of her bird form to relieve herself. She'll wait to find nourishment at the airport as a Spellbinder and not a bird.

Juniper Berry finds the large number of people moving through the airport terminal unnatural; her childhood property is secluded and the neighbouring town is small. This is her first airport experience. As her eyes dart over the crowd, her chest tightens and her breathing becomes shallow and fast like the throngs of people hurrying around her are pressing in on her. The air is clogged with cologne, cleaning products, foods, sweat, bad breath, and several other stinks. Then there's all the racket from the automatic doors, intercom, luggage wheels, conversations in multiple languages, babies crying, and other commotions. Grimacing, Juniper Berry repositions placing the wall against her back, observing and studying how everything inside the terminal works so that she can copy people without drawing attention to herself.

One of the first things she notices is that children don't travel without an adult. This must be why her mother told her about the passports. Juniper Berry riffles through her bag and pulls out three passports. "Excuse me," she calls to a grandmotherly lady with big pearl earrings and too much perfume.

The lady stops and stares.

Juniper Berry tries to smile, but can't help feeling

like she's snarling instead. "Do you know if I can go through there," she points to the security desk, "with my parent's passports and wait for them on the other side?"

The lady is wagging her head back and forth the whole time Juniper Berry is talking, and the extra skin on her chin moves independently of her head. She tuts at Juniper Berry and surveys her. Her eyes narrow. "No, you cannot, young lady. Where are your parents?"

Juniper Berry points in the opposite direction from the lady. "That's my mother over there. Guess I don't need to wait." She hurries into the crowd in front of the check-in counter and gets swept along. In a sea of people whose foremost concerns are their own activities, Juniper Berry isn't worried about using her magic. Besides that, most normies don't see magic anyway. Before she reconsiders, her flesh tingles and stings, and she's standing with the attendant, passing her mother's passport forward and buying a plane ticket.

"Thank you, Mrs. Juniper. You can head to security that way." The attendant doesn't give her a second glance as she calls to the next client waiting in line.

When Juniper Berry clears the security counter, she's shaking and nauseous from the strain of everything. She brushes the first tear from the corner of her eye, hoping that nobody is watching her. Another tear follows, and another. She bows her head and runs to the first washroom she sees. She veers past the woman's restroom and cranks open the door to the family lavatory, locking it shut behind her. Eyes closed, she slumps against the door until her shaking subsides and her insides settle.

She opens her eyes. The individual staring back in the mirror is more than she can bear and her stomach churns. Her mother's brown eyes, with their faint hint of crow's feet, are peering at her from where her own eyes should be. She scans herself, holding her mother's persona like an outfit that can be removed at will.

Her stomach rolls and its contents tear from her body. The sour stench of bile lines her nasal passage and her mouth feels curdled and pasty. She spits into the toilet and wipes her lips across the back of her hand. When she stands and peers in the mirror, she sees her own pale brown eyes and cinnamon hair. Reaching behind her, she pulls her long hair forward and strokes her three-braid ponytail.

The handle on the bathroom door rattles but holds closed. Juniper Berry places her hands on the cold, solid surface of the sink and pushes her spine tall. She swipes at her eyes to clear away the last of the wetness. Steeling herself, she reaches toward the tingling sting and resumes the disguise of her mother.

"It's okay, Juniper Berry," she tells herself in her mother's voice while wearing her mother's face. "I love you." She shuts her eyes and directs her hand to stroke her cheek like her mother used to do. With that, she marches out of the bathroom to the gate where her plane is already boarding. In no time, she's seated and thousands of feet in the sky.

Juniper Berry can't help but compare flying on a plane to soaring on her own wings. She appreciates the height a plane can achieve, but the bumps, drops, and seatbelt restrictions add nothing to the experience. The patch of turbulence that has the plane swaying and people scurrying to their seats is terrifying.

Perhaps Juniper Berry is over-sensitive to her lack of control, but the wide eyes of other passengers with their hands gripping the seat arms suggest otherwise. The recycled air smells like strange food and sweaty human flesh. She longs to stretch her own wings but knows she lacks the wing strength to complete a flight from one side of the country to the other. She chooses to sleep. Since she shed her mother's skin while on the plane walkway, she isn't struggling to control and hold her newfound magic. If she doesn't draw attention to herself, no one is likely to question her about who she's travelling with.

It's nighttime when the plane reaches Canada's east coast. Juniper Berry's senses are alive as she walks out of the doors of the airport. The salty air sits heavy, perfumed with algae and marine life, both differences she immediately notices. It captures her curiosity, and she makes a goal to visit the waterfront as soon as she can. Beyond knowing she needed to travel to the east coast, this is part of her journey that she doesn't have instructions to follow. In fact, she doesn't know what to do now at all but assumes it has to do with the letter. Her mother told her to stay out of sight, be patient, and help would present itself. Cryptic instructions that appear empty.

The letter she retrieved from Allurist Detention Centre is nestled in her pocket, still unopened. Juniper Berry spends the night wandering the streets, contemplating the envelope. The contents are so important that her mother hid it somewhere she thought nobody would search, and then died protecting it. Her walking takes her to a dock set by the ocean. In the black of the night, Juniper Berry can only hear the rhythmic rolling of the waves. She sits on the bench with the envelope in her hand, running her finger along the unbroken seal, tracing the bumpy waxiness.

When her brain shivers, Juniper Berry doesn't panic like she did in her parents' house. The momentary trembling precedes the change in her vision. Everything in her line of sight blurs. She tips her head down and closes her eyes to control the nausea. The image dances for her, as real as if she is living it, and the emotion it creates threatens to overwhelm her: a feeling of family, love, and loss. Juniper Berry is shown that chunks of her life will be connected to the streets and an encounter with a Spellbinder dove named Al. Al is intertwined with four words from the vision that confuse Juniper Berry: game, flame, distraction, and fight. Tears pour from Juniper Berry's eyes long after the vision ends, her body wracked with silent sobs.

She's aware dawn has broken, and the sun is creeping up over the ocean, but she stays statue-like with her head bent, waves of anxiety, sorrow, and pain washing over her. She draws strength from being able to experience emotions and tries to soothe herself by breathing deep, holding that breath for a few seconds, and breathing it out. She imagines her unease being expelled with each breath. When she observes at least a momentary lull in her discomfort, she raises her head to the rising sun and opens her eyes.

What she sees captures her, the way the water sparkles like millions of diamonds rippling out from a centre point of concentration. What is this world, provinces away from where she was raised? She questions being sheltered, and her anger redirects. It blooms from the tiny seed of hatred and grief she swore she wouldn't feed. At this moment, it feels good, comforting, and protective, so she wraps it around herself like a cloak of power. She closes her eyes, blocking out the beauty, and turns to embrace the rising darkness . . .

Juniper Berry dies, allowing JB to be born. With JB's birth comes a purpose.

Chapter 6
JB

In a dirty gas station washroom, JB stares at the reflection glaring back at her in the cracked mirror. She sees youth and innocence, the girl her parents loved. She can't be that girl anymore; that girl has too much pain. Her image, although riddled with sorrow, doesn't portray her seething anger, but she needs it to. She grabs her braided ponytail and jerks it into the air. A scream rips from deep inside her as she slashes at her hair with a rusted razor blade from the stained tile floor. She keeps grabbing at chunks of hair and swiping at them until her throat is raw from yelling and she has almost no hair left to grab.

The attendant is calling to JB, concerned with her screaming. Ignoring him and his frantic banging on the washroom door, JB drops the rusty blade and grinds the tears from her eyes. The person peering back at her is a red-faced girl with choppy, spiked hair. She leans in close to the broken glass of the mirror. "I control you," she whispers. Her mouth twitches in what passes as a smile in this moment of transformation, as her skin tingles and stings.

When the sharp prickling sensation stops, the girl she knew is no longer caught in the mirror. "Fuck off," she hollers toward the door, tasting the foul words. They aren't repulsive to her; she feels empowered by them.

JB observes her new reflection in silence. Her mouth is a long, thin line, scowling. She's added a weathering to her sun-kissed skin, and shadows play on her gaunt cheeks. With the dark circles around her now sunken eyes, the depth of her innocence hides there, guarded.

"This is not a disguise," she tells her reflection. "I am *JB*!"

She doesn't consider the effort of holding a permanent persona. She'll do it regardless because she's JB. Striding in the direction of the door with confidence stemming from JB, she flings it open and brushes past the attendant, who is trying to access the washroom. He tumbles into the wall with shocked eyes. He doesn't move, only his eyes follow her. JB's thin lips pull into a sneer as she storms out of the store.

With no money, no friends, and no place she needs to be, JB decides that she'll start her search for the red symbol right where she is. It'll lead her to the

Spellbinders responsible for her parent's murder, the ones her vision shows will be accountable for more destruction. The street doesn't disappoint.

On her first night, she sees the symbol, identical to the one left on her home when her parents were killed. The two flame-shaped hands holding and releasing swirling wind glow in soft red magic on the brick wall beside a dark alley. The brick is rough and cool under her palm as she huddles in the shadows of a building diagonal from the alley. She's watching street kids go down the alley, but none come back out. The stench of wet cardboard, stale beer, vomit, and urine dominates the air. JB is aware of the shards of glass and undetermined debris grinding under the soles of her shoes every time she alters her position.

The alley remains silent and dark even after the sun crests the sky. JB gives a heavy sigh. Finding the symbol is a small lead, and she'd been hoping to learn something more about who is associated with it. Stiff and cold, she rises and moves to the alley entrance. But the alley isn't an alley. It's a short niche in the wall that's six feet deep. There are no doors or windows visible, and the wall spans two storeys. "They could've flown out," JB muses. Her brow furrows. "But why go in? And I didn't hear any wings or cawing—"

"Are you talking to yourself?"

JB spins into a cat-like crouch, a defensive posture armed with knives.

"I like that," says a girl smaller than JB. The girl drops, grinning, and mimics JB's pose. Her shaggy, shoulder-length black hair swings into her face, and she blows air at it out each side of her mouth. "I like that you armed yourself with knives and not orbs. It's smart," she continues as orbs flash on her fingertips. "You blend in better that way." She lets her orbs die out and straightens up. "I'm Al."

"Al? Al!" JB tucks her knives back into the laces of her boots and stands without taking her eyes off the girl. *This must be the Spellbinder from my vision.* She's younger than JB expected. From JB's vision, she assumed Al would be older, and Al's appearance is quick. JB has only had two visions, so she doesn't have much basis for comparison beyond they happen and they can change slightly. JB sucks a gulp of air and tries the glare she's been practising. The frightful taste of the air assists her face's believability.

Al's hands fly up in front of her, and she takes a step back. "Easy," she whispers. "Easy, girl. You have street fright. I can smell it on you like a baby fresh from the birthing canal. But I'm not here to cause you trouble. I'm going to help you. That's what Al does." A big smile cracks across her dirt-smeared face. "That's me," she stretches up to full height, "I'm Al. It's short for Allie, but," she glances at the trash-strewn alley, "I can't imagine I'd last long in a place like this with a name like that. So, you can call me Al." Al tries a glare of her own, but it morphs into a smile in seconds.

JB holds her facial expression.

Al purses her lips, pushing air out of them with a pfft. "Come on, new girl. It's not safe to stand at the opening of Blood Wind Alley. You're lucky I happened by here." Al doesn't say anything else as she hurries away, her lithe form floating over the sidewalks. *She can't be over ten years old.*

JB knows she should be satisfied with this part of her vision enacting itself because it's a clear sign that she's on the correct path, but she can't get past her anger, fear, and helplessness. She shoves her feelings down inside and stomps after Al.

When she catches up, JB leads out with the question that's been burning her tongue. "Why is it called Blood Wind Alley?"

Al looks at her like she's seeing her for the first time. "You really are new, aren't you? It's called Blood Wind Alley because it's owned by The Society of the Blood Wind. It's a blind alley. Or it appears to be a blind alley." She talks as if she's years older, and like JB should know what's being talked about. "Rumour has it that if you're brave enough to enter the alley on nights when the symbol glows, you'll get a better life." She flicks her eyebrows up.

JB's eyebrows furrow and release. "You don't believe it?"

Al shrugs. "Everything has a price and a better life has to have a hefty one." Another shrug. "Either way, anybody daring enough to go in doesn't come back out. You can take that to mean whatever you want."

A shiver skitters up JB's spine, and her mouth feels dry. She hitches her chin at Al. "You going in?"

Al scrunches her nose and rakes her lime-coloured

eyes around. "Listen, new girl—"

"JB. I'm JB."

Al tilts her head toward her right shoulder and plunks her hands on her hips. "Listen, JB. You shouldn't ask questions like that, but because I like you and we're going to be the best of friends," she stops to smile so big that her dirty face transforms into a glowing beacon as she waits to see if JB is going to dispute her comment. Both girls, lonesome and desperate for fellowship, accept Al's statement of friendship. "Best friends! I'm going to tell you what I hear when I listen in the places most others don't."

She scans the area and moves in closer. Her voice is low. "That alley isn't what it seems, and neither is The Society of the Blood Wind. They aren't a group that good people, people like you and me, should get mixed up in."

Without warning, Al's hand snakes out and grabs JB's. The warmth is welcoming, and JB finds comfort in the closeness of such a simple gesture. It's a feeling JB wasn't aware she was craving, and she feels a bit of the loneliness driving her anger dissolve at the edges. Al tugs JB forward, laughing. "Come on, best friend. I have some important players to introduce you to. You can't live out here alone."

Chapter 7
JB

JB and Al are inseparable for the next few weeks. Al's eagerness to have a best friend, coupled with her resolve that JB is that person, leaves no room for any other option. JB, starved for companionship, isn't aware that a bond is forming between them. She's conscious of a soft ebb in her grief every time Al grabs her hand or embraces her in a hug, but there's no reprieve from the anger that drives JB and keeps Juniper Berry hidden deep inside.

Al invited JB to live with her. Although Al shares an abandoned house with other street kids, JB never sees anybody when she comes and goes. The house serves as a place to sleep, protected from the weather. Without power and heat, it isn't a place a person loiters. JB and

Al always enter through a broken basement door and go straight to Al's room. Her space is boxy with grimy windows, a water-stained ceiling, and stale, damp air. No light adorns the space and no furniture. JB is surprised at how fast she becomes accustomed to roosting in the pile of old clothing on the floor. Most nights, the girls sleep cuddled together.

It's in the nest of clothing that Al explains how the streets are divided between four subsets. Three of the four subsets have a leader that answers to a top street kid named Lars. Lars controls the fourth subset. Al falls asleep explaining that not all street kids want to be associated with the leaders of the subset, but doing so offers some level of protection. JB understands the design and purpose and nods off, wondering about Lars.

She wakes the next morning to Al jabbering away like neither of them fell asleep. JB comprehends Al's eagerness to get the day started but JB still tries to wave Al away. JB feels heavy with sleep. Al is persistent. With JB's eyes still half closed, Al is dragging her out of the house to a set destination.

Al, full of energy, runs the entire distance. JB paces herself behind Al, not knowing how far their jog is going to be. Moving at the pace they are doesn't allow for conversation, and it's fifteen minutes before they reach an underground parking garage.

The lighting is dingy, there are vehicles, and muffled voices can be heard from a different level of the garage. Oil and gasoline odours linger in the air. The bleakness of their environment makes JB think of the crime shows her father liked to watch. She grits her teeth, not wanting to think about cozy sofa cushions, images on a television screen, or her father.

"With me doing the introductions, there's no question about your acceptance by the subset leaders, JB," Al says, not winded, but singsong.

JB grimaces. "What's up?"

Al bounces on her toes, fidgeting like her next words are uncomfortable. "Meeting the four most powerful leaders comes with a price, one that can be hard to pay." She sighs. "You're going to be asked to share—"

"Share what? I have nothing." JB is aware her adrenaline is spiking.

"A trade for a trade, that's how we do it here," says a hard, flat voice.

Al twirls on her toes like a ballerina and leaps toward the shadows. JB strains to see who is hiding there. Al walks out of the shadows, holding the hand of a tall, lean boy whose shaggy black hair is partially obscured by his grey hoodie. His charcoal eyes lock on JB, and a smirk pulls at the corner of his plump lips. JB notices two things. First, he saunters. A cocky walk that doesn't fit her idea of street life. Second, is a stab of jealousy at seeing Al and this boy clasping hands.

Al pulls him, fourteen if JB was guessing, straight up to her and reaches out with her free hand so that she's gripping one of JB's hands and one of the boy's. "JB, this is Pax. Leader of subset one." JB feels elated that Al informed her first about this stranger. "Pax, this is

JB." Al releases them and steps back.

Pax looks JB up and down and shrugs. "Now we trade. What can you offer, JB?" His voice has no emotion. It's just a dead sound that comes out of him, emptiness. JB wonders what makes a person sound so dead on the inside but realizes that it isn't sunshine and happiness that led her to where she's standing, so it isn't a far cry to assign sadness and pain.

JB struggles. *A worthy trade for acceptance, protection, and eventually information. I hope.* What can she offer to this boy who is overconfident? JB can see Al from the corner of her vision. She's squirming at the delay. "Before I can trade, I need to figure you out a bit," JB says waving her hand dramatically to buy herself some time.

Pax? Trading? This wasn't in the vision, was it? Regardless, I'm living on the streets and I need protection and information. Who better to get it from than the subset leaders? "I get the impression that you run your group like you're the . . ." JB fumbles for the word. "Gatekeeper!" *Gatekeeper! Of course, the game, the flame, the distraction, and the fight.*

Pax considers. He offers a subtle bob of his head.

"Okay, then I can give you the gift of hide-and-seek," JB says.

Pax's black eyes squint at her, distrust flitting in the background.

Using a dramatic closure of her eyes, JB pushes away the thoughts of her parents playing hide-and-seek with her. She makes her body invisible for a few brief seconds. *What's a better trick for a gatekeeper than invisibility?* This weave utilizes light and air to mask visibility. With a more complex version of the weave, smell, sound, and magic can also be hidden.

Disappearing was never a strong ability for JB, so her parents often practiced it with her as a game. She's out of sight long enough to make an impression. Al spins, laughing when JB reappears. Pax's black eyes sparkle at JB. He crosses his arm in front of his stomach and sticks his other arm out to the side as he bows his acceptance.

JB hurries through the basics Pax will need to master the art of invisibility. He's a fast learner, and although she can't teach him the intricacies needed to conceal smell, sound, and magic, she makes sure that he knows it can be done so he can try playing with the weaves himself. With his mastery of the weaves required to disappear and remain invisible for an extended period, it's shocking that he wasn't already able to do it. In exchange, Pax teaches JB a backflip move she isn't certain she'll use but isn't worried about either. It isn't like she spends her days dancing or fighting.

"Pax does street dancing for money sometimes," Al whispers as they leave the invisible Pax behind. "He's the best street dancer. You don't know how many people would love to learn what he just showed you! Not just a flip, but a twist and a kick." Al stops and wheels JB to face her. "You picked it up like it's a somersault! How?"

"Gymnastics," JB mumbles, hoping that Al won't press the conversation further. JB doesn't want to talk about her past. "Hey, does Pax have a surname?"

"Surname?"

"Yeah, you know the last name or a family name?"

Halting, Al surveys JB. She shakes her head from side to side. "New girl, street kids don't have last names. We're just like you, JB!" Al reaches for JB's hand and pulls her along with a hop-skip, JB's blunder forgotten.

JB nods and walks, frowning. "Who do we meet next?"

"Maxen, but this won't go as quick. Can you fly?" Al doesn't wait for an answer. Her body becomes a stout ivory-white bird with short legs and a short beak. As the bird gracefully takes flight, JB feels no surprise that Al is a dove. JB shifts and follows.

Maxen's group lives on the farthest side of the city. Uneasy, JB follows as Al the dove enters an abandoned warehouse through a broken window. The inside isn't what JB expected. The clean room is like a miniature banquet hall with a shiny floor and twelve circular tables. Each table is dressed with a floor-length tan tablecloth covered with a shorter black one. Six cream-coloured chairs are positioned around the tables with a lacy, dark tan fabric tied in enormous bows at the back. The effect is stunning. The tented, black fabric ceiling adds to the welcoming atmosphere with its tiny LDS string lighting.

"Just in time for lunch, Al," a high voice squeaks.

JB is so mesmerized by the unexpected room that

she doesn't notice the handful of people. The girl with the squeaky voice and a perfect reddish-brown bob with side bangs dismisses everyone except the boy whose physique surpasses athletic. He stands beside her, arms crossed and feet spread, his golden-brown eyes watching.

The girl opens her arms wide and Al hurries into them. The girl's grey eyes watch JB as she hugs Al. "Who have you brought with you, Al?"

"A friend."

The girl, whom JB realizes is Maxen, releases Al. Her bracelets clink as she advances toward JB. Maxen's jaw moves rhythmically, and the smell of mint wafts from her breath when she talks. "A friend?"

She takes both of JB's hands into her own. JB stifles her surprise when Maxen pulls her in and kisses both her cheeks. "Hello, friend. I'm Maxen, subset two leader. And this," she flourishes her hand behind her, "is Boulder, the leader of subset three."

"Nice to meet you, Maxen." JB leans sideways to peek at Boulder. She inclines her head to him. "Boulder." She stands up and locks her eyes with Maxen. "I'm JB." JB uses her quick study of people to understand what protocol Maxen requires next, and she kisses both Maxen's cheeks.

"Delightful!" Maxen squeals. "First, we'll trade, and then we'll lunch. Because I know how hard this trading part can be, I'll tell you two things about me. I'd wear make-up if I could afford it, and I dream of being a caterer."

Relying on the details of her vision, JB snaps her fingers without hesitation, and a flame sparks to life on her fingertips. She plays with it a bit, causing it to grow brighter and dulling it down again. She reaches for the table closest and lights the candle. Although fingertip fire requires a small amount of magical strength, a Spellbinder has to be taught the weave to create it. The flame has to be for Maxen because the distraction is Boulder's bald tattooed head. JB's vision showed four things: the game, the flame, the distraction, and the fight. Until she met Pax, JB had no idea what it meant. JB will teach Boulder an illusion that'll make his tattoos move.

Maxen's laugh pierces JB's ears. "Accepted! Teach me. Now, from me, you will be forever welcome at my table." Maxen hands JB a plastic container, little enough that a dime wouldn't fit in to. JB flicks it open. Inside, there appears to be a piece of already chewed gum. It's off white, with questionable chunks of coloured stuff in it. JB isn't sure what to do. She stands with her head down, staring at the used gum, thankful for the grimace she keeps plastered on her face. Her disgust goes unnoticed.

Al's hand closes over JB's. "We'll all eat together in a minute," Al says. Then, in a voice just for JB to hear, she continues, "It's a magical meal. You chew it until you aren't hungry, then you place it in the container until it's time to eat again. Maxen spends months making each piece, and very special people, family, get one."

Al deposits it on a plate. She takes a similar container out of her pocket and places it on another plate. Boulder moves to the table and deposits his before turning to JB.

"You and I will do business after we eat." His smoky voice surprises JB and she's thankful again that she has mastered her permanent twisted expression. He pulls out a chair for Maxen, and when she sits, he does the same for Al and then JB before seating himself.

Maxen reaches for Boulder's hand, then Al's, and then Boulder and Al reach for JB's. Once everyone is holding hands, Maxen instructs them to lower their heads while she gives thanks for family and friendships. JB remains quiet and watchful as everyone pops their gum into their mouths and starts to chew. Al's eyes flare at her, and she twitches her head at JB's gum. JB tries to swallow, but her mouth is dry.

She reaches for her gum. It's cool, firm, and grainy between her fingers. She pops it onto her tongue and holds it there without chewing, letting her saliva build up around it. The flavour isn't one she can associate with any particular food, but it's pleasant enough that her brain is overriding her aversion and encouraging her mouth to chew. The texture between her teeth is like chomping on silly putty, not gummy but a mix of silicone and elastic. Now that she isn't so focused on how to avoid putting it in her mouth, she can hear short, high-pitched squeaks of teeth as everyone chomps on their strange meal.

JB can't explain how, but the knot of hunger in her

tummy gives way to the warm, heavy feeling that comes from a hearty home-cooked meal. She's smiling as she plucks the gum out of her mouth and pops it into the container. She'd like to say something about it but isn't sure what would be appropriate or offensive, so she sighs her contentment and stuffs the container in her pocket.

The next couple of hours pass in a blur of information, which includes her trade with Boulder. Then JB is saying her goodbyes without knowing what's happening. She finds herself walking along a dark, dirty hallway outside the banquet room with Al.

JB braces for Al's response to the question she's about to ask. She feels positive that it'll illicit the "new girl" label, but she can't help asking. "Al, I don't understand how these subsections work. How did Pax, Maxen, Boulder, and Lars become so important on the streets?"

Al doesn't even glance at JB when she answers. Her voice is low and there's an unfamiliar edge to it. "You don't want to know the things anybody has to do to earn respect and ranking in our world, JB! As for the subsections, all you need to know is that Lars is the top and it filters down from there: Boulder, Maxen, and then Pax."

"The boss, the muscle, the family, and the gatekeeper. Got it." *Or the fight, the distraction, the flame, and the* game, JB thinks to herself. She shuffles her feet. "Al, sorry I asked."

Al turns to JB and pulls her into a hug. "It's okay,

new girl. We were all new once. Come on, it's time to meet Lars."

Chapter 8
JB

Lars couldn't be further from what JB expected. She's average and unassuming. Her long wavy hair, held in place by a slouchy black toque with a pompom, doesn't scream "scary boss." But Lars' emerald eyes are unwavering, and the boss in her uses them to hold JB captive. She's different from the others JB has met; Lars is trained in her magic and the art of fighting. Her smile is steady as she correctly guesses JB's question and nods. Lars' voice is a sigh with white noise buried in her words. "My life here started as a rebellion. I couldn't find my place, so I went somewhere I could make one and earn respect for it."

JB needs to be near Lars when she speaks to her. JB's words are meant only for them. The words are her offering. She moves as close to Lars as she can without causing alarm. Their bodies are offset. They are facing forward, so they don't see each other. Neither turns their head, but their eyes watch one another from the side.

"When your work is done here, respect for your name will linger long after you're gone. You'll return home, re-made as the powerful woman you're becoming." JB's voice is low, and when she's spoken her two sentences, she remains quiet, waiting.

Lars' gaze moves forward, and JB can tell there's an internal process at work. Then Lars eyes her from the side. Lars gives a shallow incline of her head, slowly and with a brief pause. Their trade is quick; Lars is aware that JB has satisfied trade with Pax, Boulder, and Maxen. So, Lars' trade is acceptance of JB into their ranks. Lars is eager to move on to pressing matters. She assigns them to watch Blood Wind Alley until the next time the symbol glows, which fits well with JB's motives.

"Watch, but don't engage. There are rumours that our Spellbinder street kids are being used in Blood Wind Alley." This is the first time Lar's steady smile falters. There's a heat in her breathy voice. "Their life force is being drained from them to increase the strength and life span of the Spellbinder draining them. It's an outlawed magic, that leaves the shell of their body enslaved until they literally scatter into dust—"

"Hollow people." Al's shaky voice interruption draws JB's gaze. She rushes her hand toward Al's outreached one, conscious of the bout of dizziness that attacks Al. A fear reaction. JB's response to the idea that these kids she has spent weeks getting to know, kids who are her new family, are being singled out for this unjust treatment isn't one of lightheaded dizziness. JB brims with pure white anger. It's seething and triggered by her recent loss of her parents and former life.

"For now, we gather information. We need to confirm the truth in the rumour before we make a plan." Lars' unwavering gaze locks on Al. "Watch Al. Don't engage! Staying out of the alley is the closest thing to protection we have."

There isn't anything else to say. Lars dismisses them, posthaste. JB and Al's fingers remain interlocked, warmth and comfort flowing through them, but neither speaks, each lost in their own silent battles over this revelation.

Blood Wind Alley remains dormant for the first few nights JB and Al watch it. High volumes of street kids move past. Some slow down to peer in the shadows while others move by, unaware. Al knows all of them; the network of the streets is intertwined, and survival depends on it. JB and Al don't break from their hiding spot to speak to any of them, but Al rattles off their names and parts of their stories. With each new piece of information, JB feels closer to their world: responsible and protective.

On the fifth night, the symbol glows. The pale red light starts at the base of the flame hands and creeps out the fiery fingers, reaching the winds until it's all aglow, marking Blood Wind Alley as open for any desolate enough to enter. JB leans forward as if the few inches will make the interior of the alley visible. There's no movement within the depths, no sound, no sign that there's anything beyond the short-bricked niche.

"How do you think they get in?" JB wonders aloud.

"What makes you think someone is in there? What if you go in, then through a magically hidden door to somewhere else?"

JB shrugs, her eyes glued to the alley. "I guess I hoped that whoever is stealing lives is doing it without being ordered to. A lone act completed in isolation . . ."

Silence settles over them as they watch kids and an occasional adult hurry past the alley. Al's body tenses as a girl whom Al calls Edie approaches the entrance to the alley. Edie and Al met and fulfilled their trade with Lars together. Although their roles within the street world took them down different paths, they have remained friends.

Edie stops in front of the symbol. Her backside is visible to them. Her head tilts toward the symbol, but her body remains to the side of the entrance. She tips her head down and angles sideways so she can see around the edge of the wall into the dark shadows. JB's skin ripples as fingers of cold fear run over her. A ruffle of feathers from a bird shaking its wings fills the air. JB's breath rushes out when Edie turns and runs full speed away from the alley, her feet banging the street like a death knell.

It's impossible to know if she was there of her choosing or sent for some other purpose. Edie was one of the first street soldiers JB met. She embraced JB in the same easy manner that Al had. JB's frustration boils with their inability to warn anyone about the rumoured danger. *Spies? Why would anyone among us align themselves with Blood Wind Alley and its people?*

The night air is damp and heavy with the sharp, aromatic smell of rain. A movement to the right of the alley draws JB's attention as a coolness on the side of her body signals that Al isn't as close as she was.

Al?

JB studies the movements of the person creeping in the alley's direction and recognizes the graceful, floating movements of her friend, her street sister. *What are you doing, Al?*

The next few minutes move in fast forward. A bird, likely the one preening itself and watching from the sidelines, the one that was just heard ruffling its feathers, swoops into view just as Al moves, blocking the alley's entrance. The bird shifts into a mangy-looking girl that JB recognizes as Auden. Auden has a persistent cloud of dust that cloaks her. She's a rival, not aligned with the subsets. Auden is angry with life, dangerous, and unfriendly.

There's a bang. The alley erupts in a purplish-grey smoke backlit with a pale light. The alley is about to produce someone associated with The Society of the Blood Wind. JB sees a form moving through the fog. Auden grabs Al with two hands and turns throwing Al into the entrance. Her voice is a strangled scream. "Sorry, Al. To be saved when I enter the alley, *she* said I needed to make a sacrifice."

Al's cry cuts off as her body fuses with the cloud of smoggy purple-grey particles. JB is running, unaware of making a conscious choice to move. She's hyper-focused on the form walking in the fog like it plans to breach the alley into the street. JB notices Pax's lean form as he stops hiding and begins to seek. He dances in and throws a solid punch at Auden's stomach. She buckles without a fight.

The fog parts, and a grizzled woman steps out. A cackle rolls off her lips into the air, combining with the first crack of thunder. Her long black cloak draws back behind her in a vortex of unseen wind. Her hands are angled with her fingers, making a pulling motion away from Auden's body. "A pity your sacrificial offering to me didn't endure my mist. Did you panic, Auden? Did you forget my instruction to wait for me to beckon you and your sacrifice into the alley? No matter, now you will become the offering." Auden's body is arched as a wispy version of her is being drawn from her physical form.

She's sucking Auden's life out. JB drops into a

defensive crouch, her hand a blur as it snatches the knives from her boot, hurling them with deadly accuracy at the woman. The metal glows with electric magic that superheats the blade. As the knives hit their mark, the woman's cackle becomes a strangled gurgle. JB is up and running.

The woman's hands claw at her neck in surprise, her body still standing as her brain processes this new reality. JB closes the distance and times her back flip. As her body twists in the air, she uses her feet to push the knives deeper into the soft neck tissue. When she pulls out of the flip, her feet hitting the ground corresponds with the woman's body doing the same.

The symbol is no longer glowing, having winked out with the woman's life; the alley is dark, and the street is eerie in its silence. JB is frozen to the spot, staring at the unmoving body, aware of the ebb and flow of her anger. Her blood is a rush in her ears, and her muscles are still tense. This kill was too easy. This woman wouldn't have been able to overpower Ensley and Aaron, so she couldn't have been their killer. JB is unaware of the disconnect in her thoughts as she considers her parents' deaths; not Mom and Dad, but Ensley and Aaron.

The breath from Pax's emotionless voice tickles her ear. "We need to go, JB. Nobody will question bodies being found here, but we need to leave." He doesn't touch her, but he's close enough that JB's nose fills with the mild, earthy spice of pepper that clings to him. JB senses the tension radiating off him. He hesitates behind her, but he says no more. Then JB can feel his absence. The reek of human waste, freshly spilled blood, and liquor plugs her senses.

Large, icy rain pelts her skin, welting her flesh where it's not covered by clothing. She watches the body in stunned horror because, in this act of revenge, her anger has receded, and she doesn't feel as helpless as she has since her parents' murder. With slow, pronounced movements, she bends and undoes the clasp holding the woman's cape shut. Removing it from the body, JB wraps it around herself with a flourish and retrieves her boot knives.

Pax will tell the others what happened here tonight. Her position within their network secured, JB doesn't need to return to them. Tonight has given wings to her desire to hunt the symbol. Tonight, she understands she'll kill again.

Chapter 9
JB

The unopened envelope JB retrieved from Allurist Detention Centre is in her hand. Her mother hadn't told her to open it, but she hadn't told her not to. JB assumed that the help her mother said would come was responsible for the envelope and its contents.

JB hasn't viewed the envelop since her vision weeks ago. No vision plagues her as she holds the envelope, so she doesn't hesitate to break the seal. There's a single sheet of lined paper inside. The words "Kill List" jump off the top of the page. It's clear the note was written with a specific person in mind, but there's no indication of who. Likely, she'll never know the intended recipient. JB knows it wasn't her parents. Ensley intercepted the communication at some point and hid it. There's so much involved that JB doesn't understand. Her frustration manifests in tight muscles and a twitchy feeling in her hands and feet.

Viewing the Blood Wind symbol rolls her stomach. JB's anger churns. "If I was to make a guess, my parent's killer was searching for this." Her hand crushes the paper to scrunch it tight, but not before a series of familiar letters jumps off the page. She yanks at the paper from the edges and almost tears it in half. Before focusing on the actual details of the note, she takes a few slow breaths.

"Enough time has passed to rekindle the effort to eliminate influential families that oppose us. Most, if not all, of the families that went into hiding centuries ago have come out. See the list below and important annotations regarding certain families," JB reads aloud. Her eyes scan the list, stopping at her family name with her and her parents' names scrawled beside it.

She blinks back tears and forces herself to keep scanning. Seeing that two of the families are local gives JB the next place to continue her search. The corners of her grimace spasm with an attempt at a smile. Tonight, she'll watch the first family's house, the Pickingill family of four.

The depth of her tiredness makes her body feel like a weight. She stuffs the list into her pocket and casts about for a nook to shelter her from the rising sun. Her face disappears behind a yawn, and her vision blurs with the tears it calls forward. Pulling her knees up into her chest, she flicks the hood up on her cape and cinches it tight around her body. A brief craving for the nest of blankets at Al's place enters JB's thoughts. She can't bring herself to return there without Al. Since all JB's possessions fit into the backpack she carries with her, she didn't need to go back.

JB locks onto her desire to make someone pay, stamping down any other emotions. Then even the unforgiving hardness of the bench can't combat the tiredness that follows her vengeful adrenaline rush. Sleep overcomes her in minutes.

The sun is gone from the sky when JB stirs, amazed she slept the whole day on a public bench. The hum of conversation from walkers, joggers, kids laughing, and dogs barking makes a static noise that minimizes the jumble of her angry thoughts. JB shakes her head to clear the last sleepy fingers away before she stands. She detects the faint stink of rotting garbage from the trash can flanking the bench and wonders how she didn't notice it before. "Time to fly," she tells herself before she shifts.

The feel of the wind carrying her is invigorating. To prolong the sensation, she circles the Pickingill house twice before landing near the fence line. Crouched in the shadows in human form, she watches the windows for movement. Something isn't right. For a family of four, it's too quiet, with no lights, no noise, nothing. There are two cars in the driveway, so unless they have a third vehicle, they haven't driven anywhere.

JB shrinks and starts across the fresh-cut grass. She ignores the ball of fear lying heavy in her stomach. From the angle she's approaching, she can't see the rear door of the house, but she hears a clomp of booted feet from that direction and decides that she's going straight in the main door. There's no vision, but she feels so confident something is amiss that she might as well have experienced one. Her anger wars with her fear.

She slips into the house. An iron smell hangs in the air with a faint ozonated odour. The atmosphere feels charged, like she's entered a room where lightning recently struck over and over. Her brain makes the connection: fresh blood and a magical battle. *Are they all dead?*

A flash of her own house's main entrance exploding open hits her, and she drops into a defensive crouch. The movement, plus her shrunken size, is what keeps the hooded form from seeing her. She stays crouched, watching as the form stops and lowers its hood to reveal the back of a bald head. If JB could see his face, she would witness the twitch at the corners of his mouth, his almost smile, as he aims a bolt of magic into the lifeless body on the floor, enjoying as it arches up and slams down.

"We've been waiting for hours," a low, guttural voice calls from the next room. "Face it, the children are gone and not returning tonight. We need to go before The Recruiter shows up."

The Recruiter? No way, The Recruiter is dead. He has to be dead; he wasn't watching my house. Neither The Recruiter nor his people showed up to keep us safe or enforce Spellbinder laws or—

The bald head disappears into the hood. Without a word, he moves in the direction of the unseen speaker. JB hesitates for a minute. Embracing her anger, she stands, expanding to her regular size, and runs on hushed feet toward the bald man. She drops and slides equally silently into the room, armed with her knives coated in magic. But the hooded figure is out the door, no longer in sight. "Mark the house with the symbol and leave," he orders.

JB doesn't have time to reposition and throw her knives. A force hits her chest, pinning her to the ground. The hooded figure is still visible, but he shifts into a frightful-looking bird and flies off without a backward glance. The force of the impact on her knocked her knives from her hands, and she can't access her magic. She can sense it, but nothing she tries makes it respond. It's like an elusive word drifting beyond her periphery.

JB refocuses her attention on the weight on her breast, where a fat calico cat with a distinctive patch of black over its nose perches. She makes to buck it off, but it growls and pushes its claws out just enough to make JB aware of them. The cat's face moves in so close that its whiskers are tickling her face. JB is so focused on the pale hazel eyes, particularly the left one, with its cake-shaped slice of green, that she doesn't register the change in pressure on her chest or the cat's transformation into a male, perhaps a young man. His body is on the floor beside her, with his hands pinning her. His cat eyes and bizarre, cat-like human face make his age hard to estimate.

"That wouldn't have ended well for you, girl." His voice identifies him as the unseen speaker.

JB pulls her lips back, revealing her teeth in a snarl of her own.

"Anger, girl? You need to mind your anger. Those emotionally driven responses will get you killed." He purrs in a tone that might be wonder. "I don't know who you are, but I assume you have a vested interest in this."

JB remains silent.

The cat-man casts his eyes side to side and pulls JB into a sitting position. He hovers in a crouch in front of her. "I'm going to unbind your magic, girl, so you can leave."

Whatever the cat-man did is unclear, but there's a change inside JB that's obvious now that it's gone, and she can access her magic, which she tests with a small spark of it on her middle finger.

The cat-man stands, surprising JB with his lack of height and round body. He scratches at random whiskers on his face. "I'm not sure why I'm telling you this, but there's something about you that makes me feel compelled. I got the children to safety, but I couldn't save their parents. Now leave, because I can't save you if he returns." With those words, he pushes her out the door with a hiss.

JB takes a few forced steps, stops just short of the stairs, and turns. The cat-man marks the siding beside the absent door with the same symbol that marked her own home. The sight of the symbol makes her mouth go dry, and her rage bubbles up, blurring her vision. She drops to grab her knives and finds them missing. In her wild state of thinking, she doesn't even consider using her magic alone to kill this cat-man from behind. She races past him into the house, intent on retrieving her knives to complete the action. When she returns, he's gone.

A scream explodes out of her with a force that's staggering. Piercing yelps continue after her wail ends. It takes a minute for her to register that it's the sound of sirens approaching. She sheaths her knives, shifts, and flies into the night. Her destination? The second local house on the Kill List.

The Greensmith family home is in darkness like the Pickingills' place was. She swoops in and shifts, staying low and vigilant. JB doesn't see the fat grey, tan, and white cat stalking through the long grasses. He's fast and stealthy. This time his pounce hits her between the shoulder blades, knocking the breath from her and pinning her face down, her magic bound.

The pressure changes, and two hands spin her over in the grass. JB isn't scared. The sight of his flat, wide nose, almost drowned out by the puffiness of his cheeks and mouth triggers a vision. He retracts his lips to reveal his teeth, and a voice that emanates straight from his throat fills her ears. "You're a visionary!" He nods and purrs. "That confirms that I've made the right choice for you, girl. Before I explain that, I'll tell you that this family is safe. Gone into hiding."

"Mouz?" says a voice that JB is sure is the shimmering air itself talking. The word, *Mouz*, sounds like a strange purr. His name, JB decides.

"It seems I won't get time to explain after all, girl, but you'll be safe with them." Mouz, the cat-man, transforms and races away.

We'll see each other again, friend Mouz. JB thinks. The thoughts of her vision are cut off as the shimmering patch of air moves closer. JB can't move. It's like Mouz left her magic bound. There's no panic, though. JB feels a soft tickle of what she thinks might be happiness. The feeling is foreign, more like a memory than an experience. The shimmering air falls over her like glitter, causing her eyes to close. Her mouth gapes open, and she inhales deeply, the weight of her tiredness a sudden anchor that draws her under.

Chapter 10
Rye Juniper

JB is groggy and numb. Her body is unsure if it's ready to wake up, so she keeps her eyes closed as she scans her memories. The world is silent, with no traffic, no sirens, and no rumble from hurrying crowds. The air smells woodsy, like damp moss and wet bark mixed with pine and cedar. JB's eyes fly open when she realizes the aroma is wrong. There's no ocean scent. She's staring straight up at a canopy of leaves.

Her body sways as she tries to sit up, and she takes a minute to note the hammock she's nestled in. Confusion makes her head swirl. She pushes deep into her canvas bed, trying to remember. The details are fuzzy: Mouz, a vision, and shimmering air. Wherever she is, it's Mouz's doing.

"Good to see you're awake, Rye Juniper," says a sing-song voice. "You remind me of your mo—"

JB panics. Her hammock flips, and she lands facedown on a floor of dirt and pine needles. The impact temporarily paralyzes her as she struggles to suck in air.

"Goodness, that's a convoluted greeting. A simple 'Hello, Your Majesty' would be enough. Just like your mother with elaborate gestures." The voice fades into tinkling laughter. "Stop bowing now, girl, and get up."

My mother? JB rolls over. The ground is spongy where it's covered with pine needles that prick her palms, and she grinds her hands together, grimacing at the granular feel it causes. She sits up, scanning the area. She can't see where the voice is coming from. There's nobody visible, but there's a sense of eyes on her. She swallows as she rises and brushes herself off.

The tinkling laugh comes again, moving closer at a rapid pace. A blur of colour slows at eye level with JB. It's hovering in the air on tattered but beautifully coloured wings. JB is certain, with wings like that, this isn't a bug. She refocuses on the rest of this creature, which is an inch in size. It has pointy ears and a human face with skin that glitters, but it's the metallic eyes that draw her attention, at least until it smiles. This creature has abnormally large, pointed teeth and no lips, so its smile is pure terror. It's nude, hairless, and unabashed by it.

"Now that I've scared you half to death, I should stop playing games. Do you know me, Rye?"

JB nods, trying not to let her unsettled feelings about this creature knowing her birth name show on her features.

The creature waits.

JB's voice comes out like a breath of soft wind. "Forest faerie."

"Good, Rye." The air shimmers, a larger shadow forming. The tiny faerie becomes a youthful-looking woman wearing a long, flowing, jade-coloured gown. Her sparkling silver eyes watch JB. "Good, Rye. We say of the Green Fields instead of forest faerie, but that's neither here nor there. And I know who you are, too. There's no hiding here. There's no JB, there's only Rye. Rye Juniper, once the young Juniper Berry." The forest faerie smiles, but this time she has lips making the smile reassuring.

"I don't know your name. Or how I got here."

Tinkling laughter fills the air. "I suppose you don't, Rye. I am Queen Orla of the Green Fields." The grand wave of her hand toward the awning of leaves gives no doubt that Green Fields is the forest. "You were transported here, faerie magic," she winks, "at the request of Mouz Frone. Your cat friend." She tips her head. "Don't ask more about him. It isn't my place to say, and his relationship with us is the least of your concerns." Her tone is friendly but firm.

Rye draws in the pine scent that is underlaid with other earthy odours and considers the strange way the Queen pronounces Mouz, Mau-zzz, before she speaks. "Why am I here, Queen Orla of the Green Fields?"

"Queen Orla will do, Rye. You're here because I plan to give you what you need before I return you to your world." The queen tilts her head.

Rye's brow furrows, and she shakes her head from side to side. "I—"

"No, but you will." The queen turns and walks away, her voice faint as she calls over her shoulder. "My daughter will be your guide and mentor while you're here. She'll be along soon."

Rye finds herself alone. She moves her hands to her head; her disguise gone. Unhurried, she traces her fingertips over the contours of her face with her pale brown eyes closed. The quiet of the forest lies around her like a cozy blanket. Her body feels heavy and tired. The anger that has fuelled her since her parents' murder is just a low simmer, which allows space for a distinct feeling, one the Rye doesn't want to acknowledge. It's deep distress, an overwhelming emotion that grips her heart and squeezes. When her tears fall, she won't be surprised if they're blood.

Her knees give away and she clutches the needles and leaves that litter the ground. In her exhausted state, she's sure she feels her mother's arms holding her. She cries till there's nothing left to escape her raw tear ducts, and she isn't sure where she finds the energy to climb into her hammock. Perhaps the unseen hands of her mother lift her. Rye's asleep before the hammock, a magical cocoon, closes itself to surround her.

Rye wakes to a tickling sensation on her nose. She swipes at it with her hand, but it returns to tickling.

"Rise and shine, sleepyhead. It's been two weeks."

"Are all faerie voices musical?" Rye stretches in an open hammock. "Wait. What? Two weeks! I've been asleep for two weeks?"

There's more tinkling laughter. "Yes, and yes. Before you ask, I'll just explain, because it'll be quicker." A beautiful face that's bright like sunshine and marked with a facial tattoo peaks over the edge of the hammock. "This is not a hammock, it's a cocoon. A protective covering that sustains you while you heal and places you in a state similar to eternal sleep but without risk of death. Your body is nourished and hydrated by the cocoon, but the process has left you filthy. We need to get you cleaned up." The faerie, in a humanish form, reaches in and helps Rye from the hammock.

Rye doesn't resist. She feels strong and healthy. Her grief is there, but she doesn't feel scared of it. Her anger is there, and it feels different too, but not in a way she can describe. Rye notes the stale smell of body excretions clinging to her and takes in the soiled state of her clothing. The only thing that keeps her from embarrassment and disgust is the faerie behaving as if this is all a normal process and outcome.

"I'm Princess of the Green Fields, but you can call me Zara."

Rye stretches. "Where are we, Zara? And what happens now?"

"We're in the forests of Ontario, where we live. And now we give you what you need, starting with a soak in waters and clean garments."

Rye looks at the hammock, confusion dancing on her features.

"Oh, sure, Rye, you needed that rest, too. But there's more, isn't there? We must train you to fight physically and magically. Strengthen the talents you already have. Holding those disguises is tiring. You did it well, but it was draining you. There are easier ways. Plus, you'll need to train your body to remain holding a persona if you're asleep or perhaps rendered unconscious. Once you take on a disguise, the only way it should come off is if you make a conscious effort to shift it. You'll be a master vizard before you leave us." Zara's smile doesn't waiver.

Rye clears her throat. "What's a vizard?"

Zara's laughter precedes her answer. "Vizard, by definition, is a disguise or mask." She dips her head at Rye instead of pointing a finger. "A master vizard is a skilled practitioner of disguising, which you're well on your way to becoming. That aside, there's still the biggest thing of all." Zara watches Rye's uncertainty.

In a blink, Zara has moved in close to Rye. Her slender arms encompass Rye, pulling her tight. There's a warmth in her arms that puts Rye at ease. Zara's voice is a satisfying melody. "We'll be your family, Rye. We *are* your family."

Rye's grief rises anew. Her arms encircle Zara, hungry for comfort. Neither caring about her filthy state. *Family.* As her tears fall, Spellbinder and faerie stay locked in their embrace. When Rye's tears subside enough to talk, she pulls away from Zara. "What do you mean, we're family? Zara, your mother has made comments about me being like my," Rye has to pause to compose herself, "mother. Has she been here?"

Zara's pale violet eyes soften. "Yes, your mother was here once, a long time ago." She pushes a strand of her deep purple hair back, taking a second to catch it in a disorderly bun. "Would you like me to tell you what I know?"

Rye's body tenses. The revelation of her mother being amongst the forest faeries has Rye frozen to the spot.

Sensitive to Rye's shock, Zara guides them to a grass area by the stream. The water rushing over the stones near the bank is a soothing burble as it bubbles over the rocks. The sunlight hits the patch of grass, bathing it in warmth. Zara nods to the stream and turns away so Rye has a sense of privacy while she strips and washes. The water is cool and refreshing. Goosebumps pimple Rye's skin before she moves deep enough to submerse her body completely. After about ten minutes of soaking, Rye makes her way out of the stream. Zara, still standing with her back to the water, has her arm held out to the side with a flowing, olive-coloured one-piece jumpsuit. Rye has no idea where it came from, but she doesn't question it. She slips it on. The material is silky and weightless.

"We will return your cape to you laundered before you depart, but the rest of your clothing is not in a condition that can be cleaned." Zara says, as they sink down to the ground, cross-legged, and face each other. Zara takes Rye's hand in her own. Rye feels the tension drain, her shoulders relax, and her breathing returns to normal.

"I didn't meet Ensley Bracken." Zara begins, picking up the thread of conversation that preceded Rye bathing in the stream.

Rye recognizes the use of her mother's maiden name, which sets the timeline of her visit before Rye was born and before she had married Rye's father.

"It happens regularly that descendants will return, curious about us and the world they're so far removed from."

"Excuse me? Descendants?"

"Yes, Rye, you can trace your lineage to the faeries through your mother's side of the family, but its origin is a paternal line. Very distant, but dormant faerie blood runs in your veins." Zara raises her hands to stop Rye's questions. "Faerie and Spellbinder DNA are different from normies' DNA and it can't be eliminated after a certain number of generations. So, it's been about 500 years since Silas, a faerie of the Green Fields, fell in love with a Spellbinder."

"Wait." Rye twists the piece of grass between her

fingers as she processes. "Typically, we say that a new generation is born every twenty-five years, so that's twenty generations!"

Zara is nodding her agreement. "Yes, and there have been a couple of other faeries and Spellbinder loves mixed in down that line. But the story starts with Silas. So, as I mentioned, you can trace your family line to the faeries through the paternal side of your family."

A group of one-inch-tall faeries zooms around Zara and Rye, their ragged multi-coloured wings trailing glittering dust over everything. The light, clear chiming of their laughter fills the air along with the fragrance of flower blossoms. Rye can't help but laugh as they fly so close that their wings tickle her neck and face.

"Shoo." Zara laughs. "Shoo."

The faeries zoom off, the laughter fading.

"I can't tell you more than this. Silas loved a Spellbinder named Iris Chamillet. And he left our world to live in hers, which is typical. Each generation after is brought back at age eighteen to be introduced to our world and meet this branch of the family. Each stays for a different period of time, learning from us, but all return to your world."

Rye gazes at her body and then in the direction the faeries flew off in. "Can I . . ." She's aware of her light-headedness and the weakness in her legs from all this overwhelming information.

The corners of Zara's mouth curve down as she moves her head from side to side. "DNA can't be bred out, but certain magical abilities disappear. Faerie magic protects itself by falling dormant, but there are things we can teach you that regular Spellbinders can't do. Like holding your disguises so they don't drain you and keeping them in place so even death can't remove them. Only your conscious choice to change can. I'm sorry I can't be specific about your mother; I didn't know her. I'm going to leave you now. I have tasks to attend to."

Rye watches Zara stand, stretch, and dissolve into a patch of sparkles that drift to the grass, leaving a one-inch-tall faerie form in its place. When Zara flies off, Rye moves to the stream and places her feet in the water, allowing her thoughts to drift with its gurgling.

Chapter 11
Rye Juniper

Rye learns little snippets about her mother's time amongst the faeries. They refer to Ensley as a jewel of sunshine, because she was happy and loved life, which is how Rye remembers her mother. Talking about Ensley with others who loved her helps take the edge off Rye's pain. It opens her grief so she can feel it, accept it, and move past it without feeling like she's losing her mother. The faeries knew of Rye's father, but only through Ensley. Even so, their third-hand shared stories are healing as well.

Without realizing it's happening, Rye becomes part of the faeries' family, sister and friend to Zara. It feels like time progresses at a different pace in the faerie world. It's a slower and more relaxed advancement, but two years have passed quickly in the Spellbinder world. Rye has grown. At fifteen, she's still small for her age, short and slight. Her cinnamon hair falls just past her shoulders in a soft wave. The biggest changes are the ones that aren't immediately visible. It's her experience that gives her wisdom beyond her junior years.

The sheltered and stable environment offered by the faerie world allows Rye to grieve the loss of her parents. Mourning allows healing, and healing softens the edges of her anger. Maturity provides a new perspective. Instead of revenge, Rye's purpose morphs into stopping The Society of the Blood Wind. She plans to infiltrate the highest level of their society.

Rye stands at the edge of the forest, dressed in human clothes, provided by Queen Orla, and her cape. Rye can return to the Spellbinder and normie world without standing out for wearing flowing faerie clothing.

Zara wipes a glistening tear from her cheek, spreading its glitter across her face. "I'll miss you, Rye."

Rye's arms close tight around Zara, her eyes wet, too.

Queen Orla strokes the back of both their heads. "Oh, my young ones." She stands quietly, waiting for them to release their hold on each other. The faeries stand in silence, watching, their presence the only support required. When Zara and Rye stop hugging, they continue holding hands while Queen Orla speaks. "You always have a home here, Rye. When you're ready to return, we'll be waiting."

"Thank you, Queen Orla, for everything."

With a grace that barely shows her movement, Queen Orla hugs Rye close before holding her out at arm's length. "You are welcome, my child. Now, arrangements have been made for you to go to a safe house. Birdie, the lady who runs the refuge, will set up the next steps for you. She knows you're Rye Juniper, and you need a home. She knows nothing more, but you can trust her. Go now, Rye. Your world awaits you."

Rye doesn't question the arrangement made for her. She trusts Queen Orla. If the queen trusts this woman named Birdie, then that is enough for Rye.

The faeries dissolve from sight, leaving a sparkling mist behind. Rye smiles, eyes closed, and she allows the mist to coat her skin. Pulling in a deep breath of forest air, she opens her eyes and shifts. Strong, decisive wing strokes lead her away from the forest and toward the town of Lindsay, Ontario.

The summer sun is shining as Rye flies over the row of trees that shelter Birdie's safe house from view on the road. Rye lands beside the ranch-style house and transforms. The gravel driveway crunches under her feet. She alters her appearance as she shifts into human form as a precaution, an act of self-preservation. If life has taught Rye anything, it is that nothing is certain. She gives herself blonde hair, deep brown eyes, and a splattering of freckles.

"Wow, you two are the most beautiful gargoyles I've ever seen!" Rye says with a smile.

Two blockheads, recognizable as lions with grotesque features, turn in Rye's direction. The bodies of these creatures are sleek and muscled cement, boasting layers of claws on their paws, protruding fangs, spikes, and bulging eyes with peculiar, angled pupils. All thought is cut off by ruffling feathers and an owl giving a loud hoot. Rye spins to face the wooden deck near the back of the house and gets a brief glimpse of a greyish-mottled owl with beautiful white ear tufts before it shifts into a woman who is less than five feet tall. If that isn't strange enough, the woman's enormous yellow eyes are magnified to a comical size by the large, round glasses on her face.

Rye stifles a giggle and dips her head in greeting. "You must be Birdie. I'm—"

"We know who you are, dear. Come inside," says a voice from the depths of the house. "And you, you fool, almost scared her half to death."

Birdie turns in the direction of the open door on the

deck to address the speaker. She stands with her feet spread wide and her hands on her hips as if she's about to bark an order. Instead, she sticks her tongue out and blows simultaneously, making her cheeks and lips vibrate with a drawn-out *pfft*. Laughter wafts outside. Birdie gives a hoot and hops through the door.

Rye isn't fast following, but Birdie is quick to beckon her. She hops back out and orders Rye to enter with a voice of authority.

Rye finds herself in a sunroom aviary. It's humid and alive with plants, flowers, and birds of all types. The air smells tropical with a hint of must. Rye's aware of general Spellbinder safe house rules and assumes that since she's accessing the haven for protection, the birds in the sanctuary are birds, not Spellbinders. She sees Birdie's back retreating through a doorway at the far side of the sunroom and she hurries to follow.

The doorway leads into a kitchen filled with the bitter notes of coffee and Birdie's deep voice. "We won't waste time on pleasantries, Rye. I'm here when you need me, always. This house can be a haven for you whenever you need it. In fact, I expect you to be here every Sunday for dinner. But you can't live here. A safe house isn't meant to be a home for anyone but the person who runs it. So, we've arranged for you to live with Mouz. He's away right now, but he knows you'll be there when he returns. What you need to know about Mouz is that he has limited involvement with The Society of the Blood Wind, but he uses it when he can in order to provide Pearle Ember," Birdie flicks her hand in Pearle's direction, "and me with information."

Rye, standing just inside the kitchen door, nods. Although she's been listening to Birdie, she's also studying her, fascinated by the tiny deep-voiced woman with an abrupt manner dressed in what looks like an oversized flowing shirt.

"You're studying me. I like that. We know that you're quick at picking up tricks by watching. That's our plan for you, to let you learn on your own."

Rye registers Birdie's use of the word *we*, but she doesn't want to let on that it has startled her, so she eyes the kitchen before she allows herself to speak. "Mouz, what's his story?"

"Mouz's story?"

Rye shrugs. "Yeah, like who is he and stuff?"

Pearle, a woman with messy flowing hair that's a soft reddish brown dancing with patches of silver, answers. "Mouz Frone is the last of his family line. He's the best hunter and catcher of intel."

"Right." Rye is nodding, not sure where else to go from there. *There's so much going on behind the scenes, so many moving parts putting all of this into motion.*

Pearle stands with her hip thrust out to the side and a hand perched in the pocket of a long quilt-like cream coat with a hand-stitched pattern. She reads Rye's discomfort and interjects. "Mouz's family was stripped of power and influence a long time ago by the Adelgrief family. Mouz—"

"Who are the Adelgriefs?"

"The Adelgriefs are the founders and leaders of The

Society of the Blood Wind and they live right here in Lindsay. You'll be able to identify their house by the flaming hands and wind symbol. However, my point involving Mouz is that he's as invested in this as the rest of us."

Rye feels a lightness in her chest and her pulse increases at the mention of the symbol. She knew the faeries were helping her with her goal regarding The Society of the Blood Wind, but until now she hadn't been sure of their power and reach outside of the forest. Her feelings of camaraderie toward them feel explosive. She makes eye contact with Bridie. "Sure, but why does The Society trust him? I thought he broke free and then returned to them."

"She seems to know more than she lets on Pearle," Birdie chirps.

Pearle smiles. "We're all allowed our divergence, Rye. In the end, The Society of the Blood Wind sees what they've always seen. They see someone less than themselves who erred by leaving The Society of the Blood Wind and the Adelgrief power, but that someone quickly realized their mistake and came crawling back, even more indebted."

There isn't much else to say after that. Birdie and Pearle instruct Rye on how to get to Mouz's house and provide her with a key. Despite the strangeness of the situation, Rye feels at ease with these two women. They're about the age her mother would've been. Way more eccentric than her mother but fun, and neither woman leaves her wondering what they expect from her. Their expectations are clear.

A short fly later, Rye lands on the sidewalk beside an old red brick two-storey house. The yard is tiny for a corner lot, but Mouz has a pleasant garden of flowers, vines, and other plants trimming the house's foundation. It has a quaint feeling. The side door she enters leads into the dining room with a narrow galley kitchen straight ahead. Rye notices on the left a rickety set of old stairs leading up and, on the right, there's a doorway to the family room. Given the age of the house, she assumes the front door is off the family room with the main staircase up, but she's too tired to explore.

She almost falls on the twisted stair floorboards on her way up. Her room is at the far end of the narrow hallway past the main staircase. It's a cramped, closet-free room with a large lifting window bearing no screen. Rye climbs into her single bed, thinking about the day. Birdie and Pearle made her feel welcome, but it's clear they plan to let her see things for herself. She can't help wondering what Mouz's reaction will be.

Chapter 12
Rye Juniper

Rye isn't sure if there's divine intervention or Pearle at work when Wade Ember is assigned to introduce her to the school. She's standing outside the office, watching a tall, authoritative boy move down the hallway. Wade approaches from the opposite direction on silent feet, and it isn't until he bows that Rye even notices him. With Wade's distracting greeting, Rye doesn't see when the tall boy with brown eyes and black hair walks off.

She smiles at Wade. In response, he studies her openly, thoughts flickering behind his eyes. His contemplative nature suits his dress slacks and slightly open button-down shirt.

"Is everything okay?" Rye asks.

Wade adjusts his glasses and pulls his thin lips into a smile. Rye raises her eyebrows at him. "Let's get you to your first class. It's a half day. I've taken the liberty of checking your morning schedule, and we don't have any of the same classes." He's walking, and Rye matches his pace so they can walk together. "Your morning classes are all in this hall. Your locker is there," he says, pointing to the far end of the corridor. "Washrooms are out those far doors and down that hallway. I'll meet you at the office after morning classes. Good luck, Rye." He bows—one of his personality quirks—and walks off.

Rye sighs and scans the hall. The hallway is a cluster of activities with just minutes till the first bell rings. She stands there, allowing bodies to flow around her like she's a rooted obstacle in a stream. Nobody pays her any mind. The voices are a solid, indistinct drone marked with laughter and teasing as students scurry to their classes. Lockers bang, cell phones bing with notifications, and finally, the bell sounds. Rye moves to her class without going to her locker. She takes a seat at the back and allows the pattern of school life to start building familiarity for her.

She tries to draw as little notice as possible this first day and remains quiet in her morning classes, acknowledging roll call and trying to identify names and students with whom she might want to align herself. When her last class of the morning ends, she heads to the office after a fast stop at her locker to dump off her notebook and assigned textbooks.

Wade approaches with his nose in a novel and stops beside her without looking up. Rye studies him freely. Someone clearing their throat draws Rye's attentiveness from Wade.

A plump girl with honey-brown hair is smiling at her. "You must be the new girl. I'm Cora Alden, and this is my main squeeze, Wade Ember."

"I'm Rye. Nice to meet y—"

"I adore Cora's eyes, too," Wade says.

Puzzled by Wade's random comment, Rye turns her attention to him. He isn't paying attention to Rye or the conversation. Wade, with a silly grin, is beaming at Cora.

Rye feels a bit surprised by this girl's gold-rimmed hazel eyes and her intellectual boyfriend, but Rye's learned to be a master at schooling her emotions and responses. She flicks her long hair behind her, cursing the new V-shaped layers as half of her hair slides forward over her shoulder. "Your eyes are unique, Cora. Does anyone else in your family have the same colour eyes?"

Wade stretches his spine, and his posture stiffens. Rye notes there's an underlying tension humming through Cora as well. She turns to see what has caused this change in them.

The boy from earlier is moving down the hall in their direction. His walk, which Rye had assumed was leisurely, is more stealthy, almost predatory. The kind of predator that knows there isn't another animal capable of causing him damage.

If the vibes radiating from Wade and Cora weren't a warning, Rye knows this boy's dark handsomeness would suck her in. The pull coming from him as he prowls by is so strong, like invisible lines of a net have attached themselves to her for the purpose of dragging her after him. Her torso arches slightly.

Cora's hand attaches to Rye's arm.

As if the boy feels Rye's focus on him break, he turns and fixes his intense stare on Rye. Her conscious mind knows that his look was fast and fleeting, but her subconscious has a different response, causing her sight to soften and her brain to shiver. In that brief vision, she sees this boy's fascination with her ability to resist him and the interest that'll grow from it. Rye moves her tongue in her mouth, trying to return moisture to it. "Who is that?"

"Nekane Adelgrief." Cora remains holding onto Rye's arm. She pulls, leading Rye to the school's exit. "He's the embodiment of immorality and wickedness. His name means sorrow." Wade hooks arms with Cora. They fall into silence, grinning idiotically at each other.

"Lovebirds, where are we going?"

"Home. And you're coming." Cora says. "You need a friend; I can smell it on you. I need one, too." Rye can see the smile on Cora's face even though she doesn't peek her way.

The exchange is an echo of Rye's introduction to Al. Rye closes her eyes and lets Cora lead her while she hugs her memories of Al close. She opens her eyes when she feels a stirring of protectiveness surfacing.

Before she can give it any consideration, she's distracted by a boxy red brick house with an elaborate covered porch. The flames and wind symbol mark this house. Rye's feet root her to the sidewalk, which causes a chain reaction, stopping Cora and then Wade.

Cora releases Rye's arm. She and Wade continue down the sidewalk. Rye views the house a few seconds longer and hurries to catch up to them. "Who lives there?"

"Two guesses," Cora says.

Rye peeps backwards. "Nekane Adelgrief."

"The Society of the Blood Wind," Wade adds quietly.

"Sorry, so not Nekane?"

Cora reaches for Rye and hooks their arms. "Nekane lives there, and the house is the main establishment for The Society of the Blood Wind. Nekane's father, Dolion, runs it. So, several questionable Spellbinders live there. All those people and no witnesses . . ."

"Excuse me?" Rye's eye brows squish together and her forehead wrinkles.

Cora sighs. "Last year, Nekane's mother, Onyx, was murdered. Rumour has it she showed mercy to a half-blood." Cora pauses and glances at Rye to see if she's following. "Half normie and half Spellbinder. He killed her for that mercy. Or so they say."

"What do you mean? So they say? Who killed her?"

"No witnesses. Normie police couldn't prove anything and Dolion wouldn't allow The Recruiter inside and—"

"The Recruiter is still alive? Isn't he a million years old?" Rye's mind flashes to her parent's murder. The

Recruiter hadn't shown up to help her then or anytime since. She pushes aside the anger that stirs when she thinks of The Recruiter being alive and not coming to her aid and refocuses on Wade and Cora.

"Non-issue, Rye," Wade says, with his eyes fixed on the sidewalk. "The truth of his age is a mystery, but his trick is that a limited few know his identity, so when he passes the title of The Recruiter on to the next generation, nobody is the wiser. So, who is there to say it's someone new running the show? On top of that, he's been a one-man team for years and will take in someone new when it's time to retire."

"You sound pretty sure." Rye eyes Cora when Wade doesn't respond.

Cora shrugs. "Anyway, they killed her in the house, but nobody saw or heard a thing. Rumour has it, Dolion killed Onyx in front of Nekane to make sure Nekane understands the lesson of no mercy. Nekane is different now. I mean, he was always . . . villainous, but now he's abominable."

When she hears about Onyx's murder, Rye's hands clench into fists, creating a biting pain where her nails dig into her palm. She has to work to unclench her hands, leaving her fingers feeling restless. *Poor Nekane. Not only losing your mother, but being forced to watch, too . . .*

The rest of the walk is silent. Cora and Wade pull Rye straight up the walkway and toward a grand, aged brick house. She doesn't have time to appreciate the Gothic Victorian structure of it. They enter a foyer facing a staircase. To the left is a family room filled with bright light from the five windows that mark each wall of the octagon-shaped room.

The aroma of delicious foods hangs in the air.

"Dinner," the familiar voice of Pearle Ember calls.

The clacking of boots draws Rye's inquisitiveness to the stairs. A girl whose pale skin is heightened by her witch-ish black dress is ascending in their direction. She's pulled her hair back in a bun so tight that it has to be responsible for this girl's nose being angled high in the air. Her spine is poker straight. She flicks green-brown eyes at them and walks by with a cackle.

"That's Rune, Wade's older sister," Cora explains. She cups her hands around her mouth, "Coming, Mother Pearle." She opens her hands, and a faint bubble floats down the hall. "Voice bubbles. They're so much better than yelling."

Wade releases Cora and rolls his hand in an after-you gesture. Cora tugs Rye down a long hallway, past a powder room, and into the kitchen with a library attached to it on the left. The kitchen is empty, and Cora steers Rye through the room, away from the library. A receding staircase on the right leads up. On the far side of these stairs is a doorless entry leading into the dining room. The dining room mirrors the family room, and Rye realizes they've travelled through the house to the front again.

Rye keeps her face neutral when she sees Pearle seated at the table. She flicks her eyes to Rune. Rune has an apple in her hands. She's whispering to it, causing the colour of its skin to slip through the colours of the rainbow.

Pearle's voice draws Rye's attention. "Hello, Cora. Who's your new friend, Wade?" Pearle pretends as if she and Rye have never met, presumably to guard Rye's secrets. Although, if Rye was betting, she would wager the act protects more then Rye.

"Rye Juniper," Wade says. "Rye, this is my mother Pearle and my father Ian."

Ian has the look of someone battling a terminal illness. *Cancer?* He's marked with tiredness that rest won't combat, pale dry skin, thinness, and laboured breathing. There's a pain to the greeting smile he gives Rye. He says nothing. Rye smiles and nods her own hello, noting the small pile of pills on a napkin beside his plate.

"Well, have a seat, Rye, and dig in. If these two brought you home, you're family now," Pearle says.

Chapter 13
Rye Juniper

In the weeks that follow, the Ember family house becomes a second home for Rye. She has her Sunday dinners at the safe house with Birdie and Mouz, when he isn't off hunting and catching intel. Mouz and Rye's relationship is strange but pleasant. It's a dynamic that alternates between big brother and little sister, and father and daughter. At least four of the other six nights a week, Rye is at the Ember family house. She feels gifted to find herself in a place where she's surrounded by so many amazing people who accept her as their own.

Regardless, Rye doesn't lose focus on her mission. If anything, she's clear-headed and confident. She adopts some of Mouz's techniques by watching and questioning him, and she uses them to gather intel of her own. She learns his ways of moving, as well as ways to conceal herself and ways to hear and see things from a distance. These techniques used by Mouz are both with and without magic. She also learns ways to leverage people for information. Without ever having entered the Adelgrief house, she knows the layout. She knows who within the school is part of Nekane's inner circle, a circle that accesses The Society of the Blood Wind. And from studying Nekane, she's building an understanding of the rules that govern their society. Now she needs a plan to get inside, but just like that, the school year ends.

Rye spends her summer hanging out with Cora, Wade, and their friend group. Because of the hostility between The Society of the Blood Wind and non-Society Spellbinders, Rye doesn't make direct contact with Nekane or any of The Society of the Blood Wind. She learns about Nekane and his friend group through her furtive surveillance as the summer rushes through to fall.

It's the last night of the summer before a new school year starts. The breeze carries nostalgia as Rye swoops into the sunroom at Birdie's place. She shifts mid-air and lands in a crouch. The fragrant aroma of fried onions and the offensive stink of cooked liver mixes with the birdhouse smells. A ghost of the liver's texture profile, creamy and soft, awakens Rye's taste buds. Her eyes survey the room for the voices she hears. Birdie's voice is moving closer from the kitchen. "We have to stop them, Quinlan, before things get too far out of hand. We—"

Rye stands, cutting off Birdie's conversation as she enters the room. There's a man with Birdie that Rye recognizes as someone she's seen leaving here before. She's also seen him in Pearle's company.

Birdie hoots and puts a hand over her heart. Her wide eyes flash with surprise. "Rye, you're early."

Rye smiles at Birdie before directing her attention to the man. His bald head, flat face, and smooth skin give him an ageless quality, but his eyes give him away. They twinkle with a deep knowledge that's earned through age and experience.

For Rye, there's something more to this man. Excited, she leans forward. He's a vizard. So few Spellbinders can alter their appearance and hold it for extended periods like she can. She can't say why she knows Quinlan is doing this. She isn't gifted with the ability to see threads of magic, but she knows he isn't showing his true self. Without a way to contact the forest faeries, Rye is restricted to wishing she could ask Zara. It seems reasonable that Rye sensing this man's disguise is something from the magic the faeries helped her shape. He has modified his appearance to navigate the telltale signs of age.

"I know who you are," she says before she thinks better of it.

Quinlan says nothing. Birdie and the birds have fallen silent.

Rye nods, giving herself permission to move forward. "I know that bird is with you," she continues with her finger thrust toward a small hawk with a long tail and short, round wings. "I'd say that bird is your protégé, apprentice, trainee, or whatever you call it. You're The Recr—"

Quinlan gives a booming laugh. "Enough. You've made your point. What is it you want?" There's no anger or concern in his voice. He sounds amused and pleased with her ability to discern his identity. *Could he have wanted her to know, or is there something unseen at play?*

Rye flicks her head between Quinlan, the hawk, and Birdie.

"No time to doubt yourself now, Rye. Out with it." Birdie orders. Dinner is forgotten.

"I'm going to infiltrate The Society of the Blood Wind, and I've a plan." Her words come out in a rush. The silence that follows is cold and heavy. Rye feels a tinge of anger and regrets choosing to say anything when she could've just set her ploy in motion.

"No." Birdie doesn't blink her owl-like eyes; she just stares.

Heat flashes through Rye's body, and her muscles

quiver. Rye returns Birdie's stare through slitted eyes. "I have an interest vested in this that's personal, and I'm doing this."

Birdie crooks a finger at Rye. "No, you aren't." She makes a series of tweets and chirps, and a plump bird with blueish-grey feathers swoops down onto the table. Its head moves back and forth with jerky movements as its orange eyes study Rye. Birdie gives a couple more chirps. The messenger bird, not a Spellbinder—some birds are just birds—flies out of the sunroom. Birdie rips her eyes from Rye in a way that suggests she no longer sees her and focuses on Quinlan. "I've sent for Pearle."

Quinlan nods his head. "Rye, my job typically is as a watcher without direct involvement. I watch, assess, gather information, recruit when necessary, and organize missions for my recruits. So, I'm not sure what you are asking?"

Rye repositions so that she can't see Birdie. "I need someone to help me. Watch me, I guess, in case things get too difficult. I've been watching and assessing as well, and I know I can get accepted into The Society of the Blood Wind through Nekane Adelgrief.

"Once I'm in, I'm unsure what to do. When I gather intelligence, I need someone to give it to. Someone who'll know what to do with it." She pauses and swallows. "There was a time when I would've gone and killed as many of them as I could, but something more effective needs to be done to end The Society completely, and not just allow for someone new to lead their charge."

Quinlan nods. "Recruits and their projects don't involve infiltrating The Society of the Blood Wind. I don't recommend this course of action." He holds his hand up to silence the argument he perceives Rye is about to spew. His voice is low and firm. "I know that you'll not be swayed from your mission. And Rye, I know why. I went to your home, and I saw. So, if you can convince Birdie or Pearle to be your handlers, then my hawk will be theirs."

Rye changes position again so she can see Birdie. Birdie's throat is moving like a bird regurgitating food.

Quinlan nods to her. "Goodbye, old friend." He doesn't wait for a response. He shifts into a gyrfalcon and hauls his thick, powerful body out of the house on pointed wings.

The hawk remains perched in the foliage, watching Birdie and Rye try to stare each other down. The crunch of gravel in the driveway signals someone's arrival in a vehicle. A vehicle door slams, and hurried feet cross the driveway.

Pearle kicks the door to the sunroom open and marches in. "Is this about revenge?"

Rye and Birdie both gape at her. Rye shakes her finger between Pearle and Birdie. "Do you mean this or my plan?"

Pearle rolls her eyes. "Rye Juniper, you aren't a solo teenager in my life. You know what I mean. And you," she narrows her eyes at Birdie, "zip it."

Birdie gives a hoot and hops forward like she's

challenging Pearle to a pecking match. They eye each other up and down and burst out laughing. Once they have composed themselves, they turn to face Rye as a united front.

Rye isn't cowed by them. She steels her spine and straightens as tall as she can. "I'm doing this, ladies. I appreciate everything you've done for me, but this plan is the whole reason I'm here. Tell me there isn't something more going on. Besides, I'm your best bet to get a handle on whatever it is. I'm not asking your permission. I'm asking for your help."

Birdie and Pearle exchange a knowing look. "By getting in *through* Nekane, do you mean you plan to become one of his . . ." Birdie's voice fades out as she struggles for a word.

"Whore?" Pearle, in a monotone, asks Birdie.

Birdie chokes on a chirp. She coughs and sputters. "Not what I was going to say, Pearle. Girlfriend or groupie?"

Satisfied with their question, they turn to Rye.

"Girlfriend," Rye says.

"No sex!" Birdie orders.

"No sex," Pearle echoes. She shakes her head. "That's not a sentence I ever thought I would say."

"Pearle!" Birdie hoots.

"What? Oh, it's a sentence I firmly mean in relation to Rye. But for myself, I—"

Rye clears her throat. "So. You'll help me?"

"Not because we want to, Rye. This is not something either of us thinks you should do." Birdie sighs. "To keep you safe, we'll do it." She says, moving in to hug Rye.

"For your parents," Pearle says, drawing an eyeball from Birdie and leaving Rye curious about how much they've dug up about her and her past. "Later," Pearle mouths.

"Thank you," Rye whispers, tears streaking her cheeks.

The tiny hawk squawks and flies out of the house with the answer he'd been waiting for.

Rye is standing outside the Ember family house, using the shadows to hide. Pearle promised she would help Cora with the sting of what'll appear to her as Rye's betrayal. Cora's safety requires that she doesn't know of Rye's plan or Pearle's part in it. "I'm doing this to keep you safe, to keep us all safe," Rye whispers, even though Cora isn't around to hear.

"There are other choices, Rye," a hoarse voice says.

Rye jumps and takes a defensive stance, knives in her hands laced with her favourite magic. But the boy, perhaps older than her, puts her at ease just by being present. There's something about him that feels familiar. Rye can't be certain, but she thinks he's The

Recruiter's protégé. He's a short, thickset boy with broad shoulders and he presents like a sturdy tree in a windstorm. "There are other choices," he repeats.

Rye can't keep the pained expression from crossing her features. "Not for me."

He nods and takes a step forward. He watches her, searching her face. She notes his strange, dark brown eyes dotted with black specks. "Have you seen me before?" he asks.

His questioning expression makes Rye think he's referring to her visions, but the faeries are the only ones who know about her ability. She shakes her head dismissing the idea and answers the boy's question.

"That's okay. Be safe, Rye Juniper, and know that I'll be watching." He turns and walks away without looking back and he doesn't transform into a bird. He gives her no hints about who he is.

Her vision comes when he's out of sight. It isn't really a vision, but a whispered name that makes her feel safe and loved. *Cian.* She pushes it out of her mind, knowing there's no time for it now. She has a mission to set into action.

Chapter 14
Rye Adelgrief

The waxy turpentine scent from the polished floors lingers in the school. It's clear that no amount of waxing will remove the floor scuffs, which is good because they pair well with the dirty white, dented lockers. It's the first morning of school. Rye positions herself where she knows the scene she's about to cause will catch Nekane's attention. Her heart is beating hard when she hears Cora chatting away, presumably with Wade. Rye keeps her eyes down, pretending to read a book, while she works to regulate her breathing. She ignores Cora's throat clearing.

Cora stomps her foot, "Rye?"

Rye arranges her facial features. With narrow eyes, a scrunched-up nose, and her lips pulled tight against her teeth, she lifts her head to glare at Cora.

Cora retreats a step and raises a hand to her chest. "Rye, what's wrong?"

"What's wrong?" Rye parrots infusing her voice with a venomous tone. She fixes her eyes on Cora and increases her volume until she's yelling. "What's wrong? I'll tell you what's wrong, little Miss I'm-so-perfect, little Miss I'm-dating-a-member-of-the-Ember-family. What's wrong is that you're dating a member of the Ember family. You've let yourself fall so far you can't see they stand for everything that's wrong with our kind."

Rye pulls herself upright as Cora's hand flies up to cover her own mouth in surprise. She's careful to leer at Cora. Any distraction, especially seeing Wade, could crush her façade. "Don't you ever dare to talk to me again, Cora!" With that, Rye spins in Nekane's direction and, as she walks by him, she casts a peek at him out of the corner of her eye and winks.

Rye doesn't dare stop walking until she reaches her first class. Sliding her body into a desk at the very back of the room, she crosses her arms, hoping the pools of sweat under her breasts won't soak through when she uncrosses them. She keeps a scowl pasted on her face for fear that if she lets it slip, her tight grip on her emotions will crumble. She's sure a piece of her heart chipped off and fell away as she experienced the hurt and confusion in Cora's eyes. *This is to keep you safe, Cora.*

Rye is relieved the sinking feeling in her stomach

isn't visible outside her body. She notices a subtle change in the air, hungry energy. Her skin prickles as if intense eyes are focused on her. She remains locked in her closed-off posture, glaring forward, but she knows Nekane has paused in the doorway. He's assessing her.

When he's moved on to his classroom and the weight of his stare is gone, Rye allows her scowl to fade and leans her crossed arms on her desk to support her body. She feels heavy. She breathes out a hefty sigh. Step one is set in motion.

Rye avoids Cora and Wade for the rest of the week, which isn't too complicated since they're avoiding her, too. Rye feels confident that Pearle has a hand in Cora and Wade's response, or non-response, to her outburst. She's thankful because she doesn't think she could've relived the experience. As it is, she spends every night that week in her tiny room at Mouz's house, crying.

In the blink of an eye, she finds herself with no friends and no family. Mouz is away. She can't go to the Ember family house. She can't go to Bridie's because she isn't sure if Nekane or one of his people are watching her. From what she knows of Nekane and The

Society of the Blood Wind, someone *is* watching. Being connected to Mouz will either be a hindrance or an advantage—that remains to be seen. So, she hides indoors and cries, grateful each morning that she can use her magic to hide her puffy red eyes.

Rye is sitting on the stairs outside the school on Friday afternoon. She's tracing the cold gravelly contours of the cement and dreading a lonely weekend when a shadow falls over her. Rye turns to find a chesty girl with frizzy hair and black lipstick chomping on her gum and glaring at her. *Lori Cleo, an innermost of The Society of the Blood Wind.*

Lori gazes away, searching like there has to be some better way to occupy her time. Her head makes narrow movements back and forth. "He wants you," Lori says in a bored voice. She turns to go up the stairs but stops. Using her hands, she adjusts her breasts. She huffs and marches into the school.

"Go time," Rye says to herself. She doesn't hurry after Lori. She takes her time in a show of power. She remembers that first day when she resisted the pull of Nekane's predatory energy, the way he had looked at her: fascination. If she has read him properly, by offering him a challenge—something more than a plaything role offered by girls before her—she'll earn her ticket inside The Society of the Blood Wind.

Lori—annoyed with Rye's unhurried response—is standing in the middle of the hallway, tapping her foot and twirling strands of hair. Her jaw is moving so furiously against the gum in her mouth that her tongue will get bitten clear off if it impedes her teeth.

Rye doesn't even flick her eyes Lori's way. Rye strolls by her and continues in the opposite direction of Nekane. She can feel his eyes on her. The feeling is growing stronger by the second. She smirks and schools her features.

"Rye?" A low voice fills the hallway.

Rye stops and turns, angling her head so she makes direct eye contact with Nekane. His brown eyes twinkle, and he runs a hand through his thick black hair in a manner that suggests nerves, not something she has observed in all her time studying him. She smiles. "Nekane, right?"

"You know who I am."

"Okay." Rye gives a half-hearted shrug, feigning indifference.

She watches him consider his next words. He isn't someone who asks for anything, but she can see his conclusion reorder his handsome features. He dips his head to hide his struggle. "I'd like to take you to dinner."

There's a fluttering in Rye's stomach. She raises her eyebrows and smiles. "Is there a question in there somewhere?"

His head snaps up, and danger flashes in his eyes. "Can I take you to dinner?"

She bobs her head down and up with her smile still in place.

Chapter 15
Rye Adelgrief

There's no surprise when Nekane pulls up in front of her house, driving a black muscle car. Rye's unsure if Nekane is aware of the three-, almost four-year age difference between them. At barely sixteen, Rye doesn't drive yet. She pushes the worry aside as she watches Nekane step out of the vehicle wearing tactical black cargo pants with a soft grey golf shirt. He's so attractive. She glances down at her sexy little white shirt and loose black flare-leg pants. Her pants give the illusion of a long skirt, which is perfect for Rye because she's not much of a dress wearer. She smiles at him, nervous.

His brown eyes twinkle as he takes her in. "You're beautiful." He sweeps his hand out from behind him and hands her a single red peony, the same flower her father used to give her mother. The sweet floral fragrance calls to her, and she can't help dipping her nose into the elegant ruffles of the petals that tickle her skin. Nekane's chuckle makes Rye's cheeks redden.

"Are you ready?" he asks softly.

She smiles and nods. He prowls around the nose of the car and holds the door open for her. After he closes it, Rye takes a minute alone in the car to remind herself of her mission.

The rest of the night progresses like a fairy tale. But the story doesn't end there. Rye and Nekane spend the entire weekend together, inseparable, talking, laughing, and kissing. That first kiss takes Rye's breath away. She tells herself that the kiss wasn't that good, that it's overshadowed by her craving for human companionship, but the very thought of Nekane's lips soft and warm against her own gives her shivers of pleasure.

Over the next few weeks, it's hard to determine if they're one person or two. The months pass in the same manner. Rye hasn't been inside Nekane's childhood home, but she has been accepted by the teens at school associated with The Society of the Blood Wind. Regardless, she remains vigilant about the possibility of being watched.

"Wake up, Rye." Mouz hisses at her in the blackness of her room.

Rye swats at him but misses in the dark.

"Wake up. You need to go see Birdie." He flings the blankets off Rye and jumps back, anticipating her swing.

"I can't. I told you; they're watching me Mouz." Rye yawns. "I'm so close to—"

"What you're so close to is the reason Birdie's requesting your presence. Now get up, you insufferable housemate. Leave the light off, and follow me to the basement." There is tension in his voice. Rye can't see Mouz's face, but she imagines that he's talking through his teeth to restrain his tone and words.

"I'm not going to that death trap of a basement."

Mouz hisses.

"Don't hiss at me you . . . you . . . you alley cat."

"Ouch," Mouz says flatly from the darkness. A purring chuckle follows. "I'm going to show you a way out of the house that'll keep you undetected."

Rye follows Mouz through the ill-lit rooms. The darkness magnifies all the old house's creaks. As they move past the solo window in the galley kitchen, Mouz forms a dim, glowing orb, bringing the dings and scrapes of the basement's aged wood door to life.

Rye saw the stairs to the basement once before, and that was enough. She hopes that her memory of them has created something more dangerous than their reality. Holding her breath, she sets her foot on the narrow-twisted board of the first stair. The entire staircase creaks and sways under her when she moves to the next step. It has to be the original stair, just planks of wood tacked together. She freezes, watching Mouz make his way down like this is the most reliable staircase in the world. When he reaches the bottom, she starts her descent again.

"Well, I guess I'll be needing new slippers, Mouz."

"Maybe you should think ahead. A century house might mean a dirt basement." Mouz moves to an old sewer line near the bottom of the stairs and lifts the ABS cap off without needing to twist or pull it. Rye can see the threads on the pipe where the cap should have been screwed onto but wasn't. The faint odour of rotten eggs fills the air.

Rye's argument about Mouz not giving her time to change dies on her lips. Her hand flies to her face, trying to block the stench. "I'm not going in there, if that's what you're implying."

"Don't be so dramatic." Mouz has a look on his face that makes Rye think of a cat with a twitchy tail. "Besides, you can go of your own accord or I can make you."

Rye doesn't need to think about that. Mouz is average in his magical strength but makes up for that with fierce loyalty. So, if Birdie has requested he bring Rye to her safe house, then Mouz will get Rye there, whatever the cost. "Okay, Mouz, how do we do this?"

"Jump, aim, and shrink."

Rye almost loses her balance when her feet hit the curved floor. "Great, I'm in a plastic cylindrical container that used to hold fecal matter."

The pipe is four inches all around, so even at their shrunken size, they'll have to walk hunched. She moves forward to allow space for Mouz to enter. He lands in the pipe behind her. His dim light shows the stained walls, littered with bits of undetermined dried and crumbling substances. That same refuse crunches and grinds under the soles of Rye's slippers.

She pulls the sleeve of her pyjamas over her hand and clamps it over her mouth and nose. "Guess I'm going to need new pyjamas, too. Wait? How do we get out? Are we swimming the sewer or something nasty?"

Mouz ignores her. The end of the tube opens near the road among some bushes the streetlights don't illuminate. Rye sucks a deep gulp of the fresh night air.

"Can you mask yourself?" Mouz purrs.

"Mask myself?"

Mouz vanishes and reappears, standing on the other side of Rye.

"Hide-and-seek? You bet I can, but not for extended periods."

"Well, since it's a manipulation of shade, light, and the air, you should be able to mask yourself longer in the dark. You just need to use the natural shadows to assist you. Since the people watching you don't know we can exit the house from this pipe, they'll be watching the windows and doors expecting you to walk or fly out. We'll travel four blocks masked and at our four-inch height just to be sure we aren't detected. Meet me at the base of the big maple closest to the corner store." He disappears.

"Oh," he says, reappearing, "we're going east across the road. Watch for cars." With that, he's gone.

Rye masks herself and hurries east toward the corner store. The streets are empty. Everyone is tucked away in their beds. Rye blinks into sight at the designated tree and scans for Mouz. She doesn't see him, but she hears him. "Shift and fly to the haven. I'll meet you there," he hisses.

Rye wastes no time transforming and taking flight as her full-sized bird. Flying at night is peaceful, and she focuses on the feel of the wind under her wings. Birdie and Pearle are seated at the kitchen table when she enters. The smell of freshly brewed coffee suggests they're planning for a long night. Rye surveys the room. "Where's Mouz?"

"Not coming," Birdie says.

"But he sai—"

"I'm sure he did. He wanted to make sure you came," Pearle says.

"It's been a while since you came to visit, Rye," Birdie says, hurt reflected in her owlish eyes.

"You know I'm being watched by The Society of the Blood Wind. It would blow my cover to be seen here, just like it would for me to be at the Ember family house."

Birdie and Pearle both shake their heads. Rye's face is swivelling between them. They stop wagging their disbelief and nod in unison at the chair across from them. "Sit!"

Once Rye is settled, Pearle takes the lead. "Rye, this has gone too far. You need to stop associating with Nekane."

"We'll work together to find a new way to accomplish your goal and ours," Birdie chirps.

Rye decides she'll approach this like she's removing a Band-Aid in one fast rip. "I'm moving into The Society of the Blood Wind house when the new school year starts." She lifts her chin in defiance.

Birdie sits blinking her enormous eyes, her throat bobbing with unspoken words.

Pearle's mouth opens and closes once before she speaks. "Holy fu—"

"Are you pregnant?" Birdie asks.

"She can't be pregnant, you feather brain. We told her no sex." Pearle leans in and glares at Rye like she's daring her to prove the statement wrong.

Rye's anger stirs. "I'm not pregnant, Birdie. But this gets me inside in a way we never imagined. I'll be living in the house with access to everything. Nekane graduated, and he's taking on more responsibilities within The Society. Me living there means we can spend more time together."

"You're in love!" Pearle says so quietly that they

almost don't hear her. "We didn't tell her she couldn't fall in love," she says with increased volume.

"We've failed." Birdie gives a hoot and hops to her feet. "We've failed her, Pearle."

"I'm not in love." Rye stands and shoots a glare first at Pearle and then at Birdie. "Nekane will tire of me soon enough. He always tires of his girlfriends. I won't be any different.

"Now, I'm leaving. I need to trudge through a shit drain, throw out my clothing, shower, and go to bed. After I move, I'll come to visit on the next full moon to give you an update." Rye doesn't wait for either of them to respond as she marches into the sunroom, silently encouraging herself.

Neither woman follows her. "He always tires, Rye, until he doesn't," Pearle yells from the kitchen. "You're playing a dangerous game."

Rye hears nothing else because she transforms and flies away. Retracing her steps into the house through the pipe, she doesn't check if Mouz is home. She showers, taking some time to roll the tension from her shoulders as the hot water reddens her flesh. She clamps down her thoughts and emotions. *This is happening.* She climbs into bed and stares into the darkness until sleep overcomes her.

Chapter 16
Rye Adelgrief

The interior of The Society of the Blood Wind house surprises Rye. She had expected cobwebs, dim lighting, unpleasant odours, and a negative feeling. What she finds is a house that smells like roasted marshmallows. That soft warm scent also describes the general atmosphere in the house. This is credited to the staff and younger Spellbinders that frequent the residence. Sunlight streams in the windows and there's a constant hum of friendly conversation.

"Who's cooking?" Rye whispers to Nekane.

He shrugs. "Someone always is."

Rye curses herself for being naïve. Her eyes jump from one sight to another. Nekane has a firm grip on her hand, fingers interlaced as he leads her on a tour.

She feels his fingers tighten on hers. He's straightened, and a glower replaces the smile on his face from moments ago. Rye, casting about, trying to find the source of Nekane's tension, misses seeing Dolion step from the shadows of the far hallway and into the room.

"Father," Nekane says. His voice is flat.

Rye snaps her head front. The man in front of her resembles Nekane, aged twenty years. Tall and proud, but oozing evil. Rye reads him right away and knows that she needs to be careful. His eyes are cold, dark, and bottomless as they scan Rye, taking mental note of her perceived deficiencies and weaknesses.

"Father, this is Rye Juniper. My fiancée."

Rye's head snaps in Nekane's direction. *Fiancée? What did I miss?*

"Fiancée now, is it?" Nekane's father's voice has taken on a sickeningly sweet tone. He returns his attention to Rye and the sneer on his face is disagreeable. "Welcome to my home and my family." His tone suggests anything but hospitality. With that, he stalks from the room. The weight that was crushing Rye's lungs lifts, and she breathes freely, noting that the life Dolion was sucking from the space has returned now that he's gone.

Rye peeks at Nekane, unsure of what to say. Nekane is glaring in the direction Dolion went. "That's my father, Dolion." He gazes down at Rye, and his countenance softens. "Let's go to my room and get you settled."

Rye isn't interested in running into Dolion again

soon, so she nods eagerly.

Nekane's room is large, with all the regular bedroom stuff in it, but he also has a loveseat and television, as well as a bookcase full of several amazing titles. "There's a full bathroom for us through that door. I had a warm bubble bath drawn for you. It's been a long day. Take your time. I'm having dinner delivered here. I want our first night together to be perfect."

Rye stares at Nekane like she's seeing him for the first time. "I don't know what to say."

Nekane cups her face in his hands and tilts her head up. With a gleam in his eye, he leans down and brushes his lips over hers, never once breaking eye contact with her. "There's nothing to say, Rye." He pauses. Rye feels pressure on the ring finger of her left hand. "I love you."

She pulls back. Her mouth gapes open. She almost gives herself whiplash, jerking her head downward. A beautiful ring hugs her ring finger. She struggles with a moment's separation from that part of her own body. The centre of the band is sparkling crackles of opal and ruby with a shiny black metal rim on the top and bottom. It hugs her finger.

"Marry me. Be mine forever." Nekane whispers as he examines her hand. "My wedding band matches, but it's thicker."

Rye's fighting her confusion, a confusion that's threatening to become panic. She feels a deep stirring of affection when Nekane smiles at her, a giddiness when he touches her, and an emptiness in his absence. *This isn't supposed to happen. I can't love this man, but*

. . .

"Yes," she says, allowing the warm dampness in her eyes to stream down her cheeks.

What happens next would make Pearle and Birdie very unhappy. But at that moment, Rye's body and mind glow and sing. Nekane and Rye are exhausted by the time they tire of each other. The night envelops them in a satisfying sleep.

The next two full moons pass. Rye hasn't been able to leave the house without her absence being called into question. Unaccustomed to such surveillance, she knows she needs to bring the trust issues to a head. She also knows that the root of the issue is Dolion and not Nekane.

It's a week before the next full moon, and much has changed. Rye stands before the door to Dolion's study, her left hand on her stomach and her right fiddling with the ruby flanked by a cluster of diamonds that protrudes from the black metal wedding ring on her finger. Dolion was making the wedding preparations unbearable for Rye and Nekane, so they married in secret ahead of the scheduled wedding date. It added one more thing to Dolion's war of words, but it crushed his control over the event. Rye steels herself, knocks, and opens the door without waiting for an acknowledgment.

The sterile space is marked by an odour that's reminiscent of embalming fluid, a pungent chemical. Each breath tastes like gasoline. As Rye casts her eyes at all the dark wood surfaces punctuated with rich brown drapes and leather-bound books, she can't explain the fetidness. She pushes the strangeness of it aside, reasoning that Dolion's cologne isn't formaldehyde, but the implications of evilness suit him. She isn't surprised that Nekane is present, that was part of her idea. His presence coupled with ignorance of her plan is also a crucial element. Finding Cayenne, Nekane's sister, in the room is a surprise but not one that Rye is going to let slow her down.

Surprise and then anger darkens Dolion's features. Rye sees the danger there. She speaks first, using a touch of magic to harden her voice. "I will no longer be treated like I'm not part of this family. I will not allow you to treat me as if I'm a dirty normie stuck to the bottom of your shoe, Father." She chooses to use the title she was told to give him since her and Nekane's flash wedding.

Dolion's anger rolls with a spark of amusement and Rye's inside unclenches, knowing that he'll not strike her dead on the spot. She's aware that Nekane has stirred beside her. Dolion lifts a hand in Nekane's direction to silence him.

"All right, Rye," he sneers, eyes flashing toward her

midsection.

Rye fights a flash of panic. *Could he know?* She dismisses the idea; Dolion can't know because she's not spoken of it to anyone. She narrows her eyes at him.

Dolion's expression is impartial. "I concede, Rye. But what is it that you want?"

Rye anticipated that he would test her, but she hadn't expected it would be then and there. She realizes it's too easy. He has a play already in his pocket. She keeps her unease from showing in her voice, keeping her tone firm and unwavering. "I want the freedom to move around without being surveilled."

Dolion sits back in the big chair behind his grand desk and steeples his fingers. His lips pull into a sneer, which is as close as his mouth comes to smiling. Rye can feel Nekane's eyes boring into her, but she refuses to acknowledge him. She senses his radiating tension and concern over how this encounter with his father will end. She can also hear sniffling and sobbing coming from Cayenne and those noises are much harder for her to ignore.

In the couple of months that she's been in the house, Rye hasn't seen Cayenne much. When she has, the girl has been a walking disaster riddled with low self-esteem and zero confidence. Cayenne can be found wandering the darkened hallways of the house after everyone else is asleep. Dolion treats her worse than he treats Nekane, perhaps because of the gender difference. Cayenne is crumbling under the pressure. Nekane has spoken about how close Cayenne and his mother had been, and how it was Onyx who had sheltered both him and his sister from the more negative aspects of Dolion's personality.

Dolion's eyes flick from Rye to Cayenne. Rye guesses what Dolion's game is going to be. She smiles inwardly and waits. He unsteeples his fingers and leans forward on the desk. "Very well, but a trust like that is something all members of my house must earn. I'll give you this one chance to earn it now, forever, or never at all. Do you agree?" His speech is smooth and polished. He's going to enjoy what happens, regardless of whether Rye agrees or not.

It takes all Rye's self-control to not look in Nekane's or Cayenne's direction. She answers, steady and confident. "Agreed."

Dolion closes his eyes, savouring a moment of ecstasy. When he opens them, he scrutinizes with the full weight of his evilness on Rye. "Kill her," he says with a flick of his head toward Cayenne. "Useless. She's nothing but a snivelling baby, unable to detach itself from the teat."

Rye spins, forming magic on her fingertips. She sees the haunted mien in Cayenne's eyes and feels her loneliness. Rye recalls the few times she tried to befriend Cayenne and the rabid behaviour Cayenne exhibited in response: anxiety, confusion, and agitation.

Anticipating that Nekane might interfere, Rye throws two weaves simultaneously. The first is to neutralize whatever counterattack Nekane makes, either to stop her, hurt Dolion, or save his sister. The faeries taught her well. It's an enchantment that renders the other Spellbinder's magic harmless, with no one else even being aware that the two elements clashed. It's a complicated magic, and Rye had to work hard to master it.

The second is also pure faerie wizardry. It's a purple bolt that moves like lightning. It's meant to invoke fear and appear to cause death. When it hits a target, the target dies. Not an actual death, and not like eternal sleep. This death can't be detected as a kind of sleep because it forces the soul from the body for a temporary period. The body is devoid of life.

How long the soul is out of the body depends on how hard it's hit and how eager it is to return. An undetectable magic sustains the body until the soul returns. When they use this magic, the faeries keep the body safe when the soul is forced out. It's a ritual faeries undergo early in their lives to learn certain things about themselves that can't be learned otherwise.

This hocus will allow Rye to pass Dolion's test without murdering anybody, and give her time to access Cayenne's body to take her somewhere so she can't spoil Rye's deception. She doesn't hesitate, the purple bolt flies from Rye's fingertips and crashes into an unseen shield surrounding Cayenne.

Dolion's vile laughter fills the room. "Very good, Rye. Very good indeed. Mercy will not be tolerated in this family and you have proven that you're merciless." His tone changes from excitement to disgust. "Cayenne, you could learn from her. Now get out of my sight before I kill you myself."

Cayenne hurries from the room, the door banging shut behind her. Rye and Dolion are studying one another. Rye, ever the master now at schooling her reactions, is wild inside but presents as calm on the exterior.

"You're free to move without scrutiny. Be gone now." Dolion flicks his fingers.

Rye turns, allowing her eyes to pass over Nekane. There's a tightness to him, and he refuses to address her. He suspects she shut down his powers, which saved him from Dolion's wrath for showing clemency, but makes him question the power dynamic in his relationship with Rye.

Rye controls her pace as she leaves the study. She'll deal with Nekane later if he dares to bring up what he'll perceive as self-deficiency.

Chapter 17
Rye Adelgrief

Nekane waits until late in the night to enter their room. Rye pretends to be asleep when he slips into the bed alongside her. She lets him sleep near the edge, wondering if this is the beginning of a gap growing between them. When she wakes in the morning he's gone, not just from their bed but from the house, having accepted a mission from Dolion that Nekane normally would have passed off to a member of The Society.

She lays in bed, stroking her stomach. She hasn't yet told Nekane that she's pregnant. It surprised her when he suggested a brief engagement, but she saw it as an opportunity to increase her trust within The Society. Rye was shocked by Nekane's insistence that they bump the wedding up and do it secretly. She hadn't realized that Dolion was nagging Nekane about the wedding even when she wasn't present.

On their wedding day, she confirmed for herself that she was carrying Nekane's baby. Now, her body feels heavy and tired. She lets her eyes fall closed, and the rhythm of her breathing draws her down into slumber.

Voices in the hall wake her. They're muffled but have an intensity that piques Rye's curiosity. She rubs her finger over the skin in front of her ear, massaging the tragus. She doesn't have to amplify her hearing by touching any part of her ear, but she always has. When her mother taught her the weave for increasing sound perception, she explained it like turning up the volume on the television remote, so Rye imagines the forepart of her ear and the tragus as her volume control. With her volume on high, she hears the voices of Mallory and another male.

Mallory Adelgrief is a distant cousin whose parents abandoned him to The Society of the Blood Wind over a decade ago to go on a mission. A nice young man, he's deemed a joke by most of the people who reside in the house. He's always a step behind; if something can go wrong, it will if Mallory is present. Cursed, they say.

Mallory takes advantage of newcomers to the house by bossing them to make himself feel more important. "The old tunnels are to remain open. Just ward this entrance. After that, spread the word to forget about these tunnels. The new ones are ready for use." Dramatic footfalls, a stumble, and loud steps signal

Mallory's departure.

Rye gambles on the likelihood of whoever is in the hallway not knowing that Nekane is away. She figures that assuming his physic is safest because nobody beyond Dolion would question him and few speak to him unless he addresses them first. So, whatever she learns while pretending to be Nekane should be safe from discovery. Her skin bristles; her confidence in her ability to assume disguises is so high that she doesn't check the mirror as she walks out of her room, oozing arrogance. She *is* Nekane Adelgrief. The man in the hall isn't familiar to Rye, but he recognizes her husband and snaps to attention.

No matter how many times Rye changes her appearance, it's the voice of someone else coming out of her mouth that always gives her pause. It isn't any different now when Nekane's low, rough voice passes her lips. "I want to see you get it done now!"

The man, a couple of years older than Rye, pales under Nekane's order. His thin lips pull tight, and his pronounced Adam's apple bobs as he swallows. He snaps around to face the wall. Rye is expecting him to reveal an upright secret entrance, but he drops to his knees and begins a simple weave to ward the corner section of the floor. Satisfied, Rye strides away without another word. She turns the corner and scans for witnesses. Satisfied she's alone, she drops her disguise. Birdie and Pearle will have to wait for her visit one more night because tonight she wants to return to the warded corner.

The rest of the day passes at a slow, tormenting speed. Rye retires early to get some rest before her night adventure. She wakes after midnight and lies in bed, listening to the house's silence. There's one person Rye worries might stumble into this section of the house and find her—Cayenne—but Rye hasn't seen her since the incident with Dolion. She makes a mental note to search her out tomorrow. Some kind of awkward apology is warranted.

Having slept in her clothes, Rye rolls out of bed ready for action. The hallway's low light comes from the curtainless window. Rye feels the house watching her like it's its own breathing entity. She runs her hand down the wall as she moves toward the corner, willing the house to keep her secrets like it has kept all those before her. The wall is smooth and cold. It appears to get cooler as she nears the corner. She considers the strange wall display with its six-inch long, brown rectangular shelves. At a two-inch depth off the wall, they're staggered like a ladder all the way up. Rye was never certain if they were shelves or artwork. Now that she's learned about the secret entry in the floor underneath them, it's clear that it's a ladder camouflaged as decorative shelving.

Rye reverses the magic ward, easy enough since she watched it be formed, and a Spellbinder of lesser magic created it. She rocks on her heels, pondering ways to open the physical hatch. When she leans forward to press on the floor, she just about plummets over the edge. Leave it to Dolion to leave an open hole in the floor for unknowing people to fall through. Then again, there isn't any reason for anyone to be at this end of the hallway or in this corner. Rye and Nekane's bedroom is the only room in this section of the house. The entire corner is theirs. Cayenne wanders, but as a Spellbinder child growing up in this house, her parents would've made Cayenne and Nekane aware of the danger.

Rye reaches out and takes hold of the wall ladder. Flailing her foot into the opening of the hole, she has doubts about the structure, but her toes find a footing. She lowers herself into the darkness.

At the bottom, she stays tight to the wall as she turns because the blackness is so complete. She scents the air, noting that it doesn't smell stale, but dusty. A light orb flares over her palm. She's in a small closet-like space facing a door. She pushes it open and her orb casts shadows over a polished stone floor. This room is well maintained, as if someone spent money renovating it. It would be a fair assumption that it was Dolion. He likely shut this project down and contracted to have brand-new tunnels built.

There's a single light bulb visible on the ceiling. She flicks the switch next to her, and electric light shines through the room. Rye moves into the space, avoiding piled crates. Besides the spot where Rye emerged, there are three other tunnels. One appears newer—or at least maintained—perhaps part of Dolion's initial renovation. Another looks like a dirt path with questionable walls, and the last one has a soft glow. Closer inspection reveals bewitchment sparkles. Most

Spellbinders refer to them as sparkles; their powers to enchant are well-known enough to drop the identifying label. Their origin is uncertain, but it's believed they were created from dark magic by a Spellbinder who wanted to decorate her home with the crystalized forms of friends and enemies. Often referred to as the Trevils Legends, reminiscent of Evanora Trevils; the stories are historical but too old to be authenticated.

The sparkles glow, creating a soft light that illuminates the tunnel they're coating. The light is bright enough that Rye could travel through that tunnel and explore with no light orb. However, the sparkles' powerful lure requires great energy to resist, and Rye's exhaustion is growing. The danger of her succumbing to them is great. She backs away.

Beyond the implications that the tunnel is associated with the Trevils family, Rye wonders what other dangers lie in wait down here. She returns to the exit, deciding she needs to talk to Birdie and Pearle before she goes any further with her exploration. Flicking the light off and closing the door, she clambers up to her floor of the house. Sliding into the cool sheets of her bed, she falls asleep thinking about the two things she plans to do the next day.

Chapter 18
Rye Adelgrief

Rye wakes alone in her bed. There are no signs to indicate that Nekane has returned. She stretches out and resettles on her back. Deep tiredness fills her body, and her hand rests on her tummy. The absence of her parents is a hole inside her that aches every day. "I can't wait to meet you," she whispers at her belly, and a tiny area of her emptiness glows. She's going to have a family of her own.

Her stomach gurgles under her hand. "Hungry in there, are you? Let's get that sorted out."

Rye dresses in loose-fitting dress pants and a stylish shirt. She grabs a carrot muffin from the kitchen and goes in search of Mallory. She finds him swearing and sweeping up a plant that he knocked over. He straightens when he hears feet approaching. Even with that simple movement, his limbs are awkward, like he lacks muscle control. His posture is stiff, his chin tilted up, exposing his neck, and his expression is pinched. When he sees it's Rye, he runs a hand through his sandy-brown hair, and his shoulders relax. "You're aglow this morning, Rye."

Rye blushes. "Thank you, Mallory." She doesn't acknowledge the mess on the floor and focuses on Mallory's face instead. His blue eyes narrow as he watches her. "I was hoping you might help me with something while I'm at school today?" She smiles.

Mallory clears his throat and checks the grandfather clock. He crosses his arms and returns his eyes to Rye.

She holds her smile. "I would like to put the small bookshelf from my room along with the clunky armchair at the end of my hall. The chair kitty-cornered on the wall with the shelves and the bookshelf on the opposite side."

He snorts. This wasn't what he was expecting her to ask. "Why?"

"Well, some nights I can't sleep, so I read. Nekane needs to sleep, so if I could read at the end of the hall, then I wouldn't disturb him or the rest of the house, and I can easily return to bed when I feel sleepy. Plus, the hall is bleak."

Mallory's face relaxes into a smile, and he drags his hand through his hair. "You'll need a light?"

"Oh, yes, I suppose so."

He puffs his chest out. "It shall be done." He moves

to give a little bow but slips on the dirt, almost falling.

Rye turns at that moment so his mishap appears to go unnoticed. She snatches up her cloak and hastens out the front door with a relaxed smile on her face. "Thank you, Mallory."

The school day passes in a blur. Rye's mind is stuck both on the tunnels and going to speak with Birdie and Pearle. She takes dinner in her room that night, after learning that Nekane won't be home for a day or two.

Mallory has placed the chair in the hall at a perfect angle. The chair is wide enough that when turned, it sticks out a good way from the wall; the hole is behind it and the chair affords concealment when she wants to sneak down and explore. Even though this end of the hall isn't frequented by other members of the house, Rye doesn't want to risk being seen climbing in or out of the floor if someone does come looking for her or Nekane. She doesn't want Nekane to catch her in the act of coming and going either.

Exploring will have to wait for another night. Rye plans to take advantage of Nekane being away. She's going to go to Birdie's place, and she isn't waiting for darkness. Leaving a note that she's gone to the library to do research for a homework assignment, she hurries from the house with her cloak trailing out behind her.

She walks to the library and enters. It never hurts to be cautious. Dolion said she wouldn't be watched, but to protect herself, extra caution is necessary. Moseying into the bathroom, she adopts the guise of a stranger she passed on the street. She strolls out of the building and walks five blocks before she feels comfortable transforming into her bird form.

As Rye approaches the safe house, she shifts into her human self a few feet in the air. She lands on the porch banister with two feet, knees bent, and one hand gripping the railing between her feet. She waits, listening. Pearle and Birdie are talking in the sunroom, but bird noises muffle the conversation. Rye steps from the banister, landing on the wooden boards with a wide stance. She smooths her clothes and marches into the sunroom.

All actions cease, then start again, animated. Pearle rushes around the table and crushes Rye to her, stroking her hair. "We've been worried." She holds Rye out at arm's length and turns her to Birdie, who gives Rye a once-over before embracing her in a solid hug.

"What took you, girlie?" Birdie chirps. Pearle and Birdie move toward the kitchen single file. "Come, we'll chat over coffee."

"Just water for me or milk if you have it."

Both women stop so fast, like a mime act, with two women riding a train. Equally timed, they turn to face Rye. Their eyes are racing over her. Feelers of magic poke Rye's body and inspect her in ways that Pearle and Birdie's eyes can't.

"She's not?" Pearle breathes.

"Oh, but she is!" Birdie squeaks.

Rye's eyes jump from woman to woman. She thrusts her left hand forward with her fingers bent down, displaying her ring. "Yes, I'm . . . or we're married."

Birdie hisses and hops backward. Even Pearle staggers. They turn toward each other, both talking at once and stating the same words. "She's in too deep. We've failed her. We've failed our mission. How did we not anticipate this? We must pull her out." They spin on Rye. "You're out. You can stay here until the baby is—"

"How did you know I'm pregnant?"

Birdie gives the impression that she's choking on a field mouse. It's Pearle who answers. She has a soft smile that pulls the crinkles of her eyes into delicate lines. "Wisdom. You look tired, but you're glowing. Your hand strays to your midsection. There are tells." She pauses, catching sight of Birdie. "Swallow it, you daft bird."

Birdie focuses on Pearle, gives one last impressive swallow, and locks her glare onto Rye. Rye fidgets the tiniest amount under the weight of Birdie's stare, but says nothing. "Rye, you'll remain here until you have the baby, and then we'll see you both away to a safe place outside the reach of Nekane and The Society of the Blood Wind."

"Like hell you will," Rye says, surprising herself.

Birdie is acting like a cartoon steam whistle. She's bright red, with steam rising from her head, and her eyes are bulging. Pearle's hand drifts to Birdie's arm and Birdie freezes with her mouth open. Pearle directs a soft magical stream of calmness into Birdie and her anger visibly fades. "Thank you, Pearle," Birdie says.

"I will *not* walk away from everything I've worked so

hard to achieve." Rye continues.

Pearle's voice is low, like she's talking to a terrified child. "You're too involved, Rye. We're scared for you, and now your child's safety." Pearle inclines her head at Rye's belly. "It'll be best to break ties now. We can find another way to—"

"No."

Pearle's palm slides down Birdie's arm until they are holding hands and watching Rye. Birdie addresses Pearle without taking her eyes off Rye. "She's too young, too emotional, too easily swayed. What have we done?"

Rye's gaze becomes unfocused. Her mind shows her a snippet of a boy with curious brown eyes, chubby cheeks, a big smile, and an unruly mop of dark hair. Rye's heart hammers in her chest, and she feels weak in the knees. The boy, her son, becomes a handsome man who is sombre and without smiles. She feels weightless and lightheaded. Her child has a perfect blend of his mother's and father's features. He's searching for a lifeline in a sea of darkness. Rye's muscles cramp and her temperature rises.

When Rye's eyes refocus, her hand is over her stomach. Both women are watching her, aware that she saw something they couldn't. It's enough, and they know their arguments are lost. Birdie turns away, her chin tipped to the ceiling. Pearle lifts her hand to her chest. Her eyes are glossy. "Should you need us . . ."

Rye feels pressure behind her own eyes and her throat constricts. "It'll be safer this way," she whispers, thoughts of her parents heavy in her mind. She rushes on before she loses her resolve. "He'll come to you one day." None of them question whether Rye is referring to her son. "He'll need you. Please be there . . . when I can't be."

A tear slips down Pearle's cheek as Rye turns and flees before her emotions overcome her.

"We love you, Rye," Birdie whispers.

Chapter 19
Rye Adelgrief

After her argument with Birdie and Pearle, Rye is exhausted, and they didn't even get to talk about the tunnels. Rye has a lot to figure out on her own. Birdie and Pearle will continue trying to coax her away from this plan she worked so hard to set in motion, and Rye can't cope with the emotional upheaval it causes her. Rye's hormones are already messing with her moods. So, the extra emotional stress caused by Birdie and Pearle's concern is too much to endure. She knows that Birdie and Pearle mean well and that they care about her. She cares about them too, which is another reason to make a clean break—at least for a while—to keep them safe.

Rye has to finish what she started for herself, her

unborn child, and her parents. No matter what that vision showed her, she'll never abandon her son, and by making sure Pearle and Birdie will be there for him, Rye feels she has already done more than her parents did for her. She's so caught up in her emotions when she stomps into her bedroom that she doesn't notice Nekane watching her from the shadows of the dark room. It's the charge in the air that alerts her to the presence of someone.

The room feels electric, charged with dark energy. She drops into a crouch, one leg stretched out to the side and one hand braced on the floor in front of her bent knee. Her other hand holds a confusion orb. Rye assumes that it must be Cayenne, come to extract an apology. Changes in Cayenne's behaviour from dramatic and overly emotional to sullen and withdrawn suggest she's unpredictable. Rye isn't certain if Cayenne could be dangerous.

A confusion orb will cause all of Cayenne's senses, including her magic, to meld into a disorderly jumble. Even when the effects wear off, Cayenne will be tired and uncertain, which will buy Rye the time she needs to apologize without being physically or magically assaulted.

Rye flicks a wave of air toward the light switch, and when the light pops on, she freezes, her muscles taut. Nekane has returned. She understands from the look on his face that he still doesn't know how he feels about what transpired in Dolion's office. His lips are pressed tight, and his nose and eyes are crinkled; he has the look of a man with a bad headache.

He's sitting in the only seat left in the room with his fists clenched on the arm of the chair. Spine straight, he sits unmoving. Rye's stomach tenses, and she works her tongue around to try to return moisture to her mouth. She can sense his simmering anger and his indecision about whom it's directed toward. Should he be mad at Dolion for putting Rye in the position to act as she did, Rye for acting without speaking to him first, or himself for not knowing her better before marriage?

"Close the door." His voice is loud but level. Rye stands and turns her back to him as she removes her cloak, which she tosses on the bed. She's grateful that she can't see him when he speaks next because the shaking in his voice unnerves her. "What else do I not know about you, the woman that I love?" She closes the door but remains with her back to him. She hears the air push from his nostrils like he's a bull, pawing the ground, prepping for the attack. "Rye, you make me feel . . . I haven't felt love since my mother . . . I mean, since Onyx . . ."

The words hang. *And how much do I know about you, Nekane Adelgrief? I know when push comes to shove, you're loyal to your father. Your mother learned it and Cayenne has too.* Rye wants to go to Nekane, familiar with the feeling of lost and found love, but struggles with the responsibility she's assigned herself to avenge her parents. Her loyalties aren't to Dolion or The Society of the Blood Wind. Loving this man complicates everything.

Rye is stunned by Nekane's use of the word love and his reference not only to Onyx but to Onyx as his mother. Fingers of guilt dig into Rye and twist. There's so much from the last four almost five years of her life that she wishes she could go back and change, starting with her parent's murder, but she knows she can't and brooding over it won't help.

Rye refocuses on her baby. Her chest loosens and her breath comes easier. She can feel Nekane's eyes surveying her and a flutter of guilt returns. The dreams that plague Nekane have given Rye insight; allowing himself to acknowledge that Onyx and his mother are one-in-the-same person is crippling for him. Rye turns. She wants to give him something to ease his pain. With a flush rising from her neck onto her cheeks, she whispers, "I'm pregnant."

Nekane's face transforms through several emotions in a flash, landing on a grin that threatens to overtake his face. He crosses the room in eight strides and scoops Rye up so she has to tip her head down to see him. There's a warmth radiating from his embrace that's a stark opposition to the cold man from moments before. "I do love you, Rye."

She lowers her lips to his as tears flow from her eyes. Even wrapped as they are together, the distance between them feels too great and she aches to close it. No other words pass between them. He carries her, lips still pressed to hers and beds her.

Nekane, dressed and gone before Rye wakes, has left a small breakfast tray beside the bed holding a cup of orange juice and whole wheat toast with peanut butter and honey. There are two red peonies in a glass vase and a handwritten note that says, "Good morning, my love."

Rye sits in bed, chewing her food, with no thought to the crunch of the toast or the sticky gooeyness of its toppings. She's thankful that there's no school today because she's tired and distracted. Rye's plan to use Nekane's affections to gain access to The Society of the Blood Wind has gone better than she imagined. Still, him not tiring of her or taking a different girlfriend complicates things beyond her wildest imaginings. Then there are her own feelings for him.

Her hand moves in small circles over her stomach. "Can I do this?" She directs the thought to the occupant of her uterus. She closes her eyes while large and warm tears slide over her cheeks and pool under her chin.

"I wasn't supposed to fall in love," she whispers. *Where was my vision about this?* "Nekane, your daddy, is so much more than I expected him to be. Under that façade he wears, there's a kind and loving man. A man tormented by the things he has seen and been forced to take part in, hiding to keep those positive qualities safe, to keep himself safe." Rye swipes her tears away and sniffles. "How long can a person pretend before the masquerade becomes a permanent reality?"

Rye's hands fly to her face, feeling her skin and contours. She sees the warning in her own question. "I'm sorry," she says, not knowing if she's apologizing to herself, the baby, Nekane, or her parents. Her stomach rolls, and she just makes it to the bathroom when she loses her breakfast. The roasted nut and honeyed smell are polluted by the acrid reek of stomach toxins. More exhausted than she ever thought possible, she crosses her arms on the toilet seat and sinks her forehead down.

The sound of determined footsteps crossing through the bedroom lets Rye know Nekane has returned. There's a sharp intake of air from the bathroom doorway. Rye can't bring herself to look at him. She stays huddled over the toilet, afflicted with her internal struggle. Nekane scoops down and picks her up. Cradling her against his body, warm and solid, he carries her to bed and nestles her in.

Rye keeps her eyes closed the entire time. He bends and kisses her forehead. His breath is a soft, warm breeze. "Rest." When the door closes, she allows the torrent of tears to escape. Exhaustion takes over and she sleeps.

Chapter 20
Rye Adelgrief

Morning sickness becomes the hallmark of Rye's pregnancy, causing her to miss mornings and sometimes full school days. She barely passes her first semester classes, and in January, she misses more days than she attends. Given that it's Rye's graduating year, and she's about to become a mother, she feels overwhelmed because she might have to redo her final year while learning to be a mom.

Rye is sitting in the big armchair that hides the secret tunnel. She's pretending to read a textbook after using studying as a reason to excuse herself from Nekane. Rye shared with him that she hopes she'll pass a science test that she missed learning everything about. She's actually reading a book on Spellbinder history, trying to find information on the tunnels. The history book—small and conveniently shaped—is nestled inside the open science textbook. A flush heats her cheeks when she hears footfalls because she doesn't want to be caught being deceptive about reviewing her lessons. She barely lifts her eyes from the page when footsteps slow and stop in front of her.

She's been attempting to create distance between herself and Nekane and from her feelings. Between constant nausea and the ever-present stress of completing her school year, it hasn't been too difficult to be withdrawn. Rye's aware that Dolion questions her behaviour. He's a cynical and heartless man. She's heard the arguments between him and Nekane about her worth as an Adelgrief, her overall trustworthiness, and her expendability once the baby is born.

"I've arranged a surprise for you, Rye," Nekane says, even though she hasn't acknowledged his arrival.

Rye lifts her head. The shadows under Nekane's eyes and the tightness in his lips speak to the strain he feels defending Rye and their relationship against Dolion's barrage of distrust. She feels a pang of remorse and tries to force a believable smile, but she holds her silence as she watches Nekane.

"I've arranged a tutor for you. I know how important it is for you to graduate with your classmates this year." His voice is wistful with hope that this act might bridge the gap growing between them.

He waits, but when she says nothing, he winces and retires to the bedroom, but not before she sees his shoulders droop. She sighs and closes her eyes, her own shoulders slumping. She stretches her neck left and right, trying to release tension. After a time, Rye amplifies her hearing to determine if Nekane is awake in their bedroom. The sounds of rhythmic breathing punctuated by soft snores fill her ears. She sets the textbook down, tucks the compact history book into her cloak, and scurries behind the chair. In the last few weeks, she hasn't been able to find anything in the histories about the tunnels. It's like they don't exist.

To remain true to her cause and to stay distracted, she's been sneaking into the tunnels and exploring, mapping, and making notes. Her time down there has been quiet and enjoyable. She bluffs and uses studying, napping, and going to the library as her subterfuge. In her efforts she's discovered a number of controversial and even immoral things, the sparkles being only one of them. It has been fascinating. Rye has learned that each tunnel has its own defence system to guard it, which is what the sparkles are.

She's travelled the sparkle tunnel to a fork. The branch that she explored had a ladder that led up and out of an old well into a field. She hasn't gone down the other side of the fork yet because she can sense that whatever lies in wait there is patient but hungry. It's an unsettling feeling that thickens the air as soon as she takes a few steps past the fork. That exploration will be another day, when she isn't making decisions that affect the safety of two.

Today she explores one of the other tunnels. She's

aware of hundreds of bats, placed in eternal sleep, waiting for someone to disturb them so they can wake and feed. Rye uses an unhurried gait and dim light as she enters, so she doesn't rouse them.

A sudden wave of dizziness overtakes her, and she reaches for the wall to brace herself. She stumbles sideways. Her eyes see the solid surface of the wall as she stumbles toward it, bracing for impact, but her body goes straight through. She catches her footing before she falls and stands panting. She's in a steep, angled hallway that is just wide enough for a person to walk in. "We can't let this mystery go without a glimpse," she says to her bulging stomach.

Cursing her extra weight, she starts up the incline. No bats hang from above. There are no sparkles, and no ominous feeling lurks. The fact that the entrance is disguised as a wall—a magic concealment from the opposite side—is what protects this space. The air is thick with dust, indicating that this area has remained hidden for a lengthy period. Rye has her arms outstretched, moving them up and down to clear away the sticky cobwebs that cross the tunnel. She gives no thought to the spiders that might have made them.

The space at the top is anti-climatic. There isn't any visible purpose to the rounded cave-like room. Rye does note the hole in the floor, an opening wide enough for an average-sized person to fall through. A peek into it reveals darkness and nothing more, but by Rye's estimation, this would drop right into the main room that she entered when she climbed the ladder. A magical descent would be needed to keep from falling to injury, perhaps even death. It would be easy enough to fashion using elements of air and water to create a cloud that can be stepped on and controlled as it descends. Another adventure to have when she isn't pregnant.

Rye's tiredness hits her like a wave, another perk of growing a baby. She retraces her steps to the wall ladder, and when she pops out from behind the chair, the house is in darkness. She tiptoes to her room and falls asleep clothed on top of the blankets.

Rye falls into the routine of working with her tutor in the mornings in between bouts of morning sickness. The wrinkles that trace deep frown lines on Mr. Paterson's face mark what he refers to as stressful years of teaching. He's a retired high school teacher who works as a substitute from time to time.

Mr. Paterson has a few tics that keep Rye from dosing off in her lessons. His left hand alternates between pressing and clutching at the middle of his chest. At their first lesson together, Rye's thankful for having had him as a sub the year previous because she would have mistaken his action for a heart attack otherwise. Regardless, she keeps track of him in case his heartburn changes into something more. With his right hand, he gestures emphatically in between popping antacids and adjusting his comb-over.

By afternoon Rye is eager for fresh air. Inhaling Mr. Paterson's musty mothball scent takes a toll. She starts her afternoons with long walks outside alone. Occasionally, she sees a small hawk watching her. The likelihood that it's The Recruiter's protégé is high, but it never gets close enough for her to get a significant look. She doesn't care too much about it. Being monitored is something she's gotten used to, and she's gotten crafty about avoiding it when she chooses.

Rye's routine cycles through day in and day out until she graduates with her class in June, swollen with child and uncomfortable in the summer's growing heat. A few weeks later, at eighteen years old, Rye becomes a mother with Nekane by her side.

For the few hours after her water broke and the labour pains had her bent in pain, curving her body protectively around the round ball of her stomach, the strain of the last few months in their relationship melts away. Rye watches Nekane, the furrowing of his brow, his hand rubbing over his face, his repeated sitting and standing. Then, when their son is born, the worry converts to relief with a slow smile and then elation as he embraces the nurses and doctors. His face beams and his eyes glow as he scoops the wiggling baby up. Baby Belamey is happy, all smiles and big brown eyes. When Rye holds Belamey for the first time, he stops wiggling and crying at once, like he knows his mother. Holding the soft, warm body of her child allows all her loneliness to disappear.

As soon as Rye is near that squirming bundle of uncoordinated limbs, she experiences goosebumps, her chest expands, and her body slackens. Belamey is her family. "Your grandmother and grandfather would've loved you," she whispers as her throat thickens and her eyes prickle. She doesn't spend time dwelling on it because she knows they wouldn't want her to. She's a mother now, and it sings through every fibre of her body.

Nekane takes to his role as a father with ease. But the strain returns to his features. Dolion makes a point not to come and meet his grandson, another rejection of Nekane and Rye's relationship. Dolion views Nekane as weak and believes he needs to be toughened up through harsh lessons and mistreatment.

Even once they're all living under the same roof, Dolion avoids them. It suits Rye fine. Nekane says nothing to her about it, but his emotions are written on him when they're alone. Rye suspects, because the man is cruel, that Dolion is still making comments about removing her from the house. She adopts a habit of removing herself and Belamey from the house as often as she can.

Rye returns to her afternoon walks, but now she takes Belamey with her in the stroller. It's on one of these walks that a familiar hoarse voice startles her by speaking from behind her. She hadn't heard anybody approach. "Congratulations Rye, on the birth of your son."

Rye turns. The broad-shouldered boy from almost two years ago holds her with a black-speckled, brown-eyed stare. Rye can't explain why she feels as if they're close friends. She feels relaxed in his presence. "Hello, Cian." She can't contain the smile that breaks across her face. She gestures at the stroller. "This is Belamey."

When she addresses Cian by name, he isn't taken aback. "Well, hello, baby Belamey. You're a handsome wee thing."

Belamey wiggles and coos.

Rye smiles and puts a pacifier in Belamey's mouth. "Did Birdie or Pearle send you? Can you tell them I found tunnels and I'm mapping them? Can I pass them information through you?"

"Are you well, Rye? Are you safe?"

"I—"

Rye bends her body backwards, her face scrunching up as Cian shifts into a dove-sized hawk with square tail feathers, confirming he's The Recruiter's pupil. The sharp-shinned hawk flies off just as Mallory walks around the corner.

Rye feels as if something is crushing her chest, and she struggles to get air. *You're panicking. Stop.* She wants to believe that he couldn't have seen her talking to Cian, but Mallory is peering into the sky in the direction Cian just flew. *Mallory must have seen something.* Rye's clutching the stroller handle and fighting the urge to look the same way, fearful that

Mallory will become suspicious. As it is, she's concerned that he showed up. Tripping over the random raised sections of the sidewalk draws his attention to Rye.

"Out for a walk, I see." Mallory is awkwardly shuffling from foot to foot.

"Is everything all right, Mallory?" she asks, schooling her voice and emotions.

He clears his throat, crossing and uncrossing his arms. "Yes, of course."

Rye paints a mock smile on her face. "Well, I was just returning home. Would you like to join me?" She starts walking, not waiting for a response, but she doesn't miss his eyes as they drift skyward one more time. Rye doesn't doubt that Mallory, in his desperation for approval—Dolion's in particular—, will report her actions. It doesn't matter how nice she is to him because he craves Dolion's favour. Rye suspected since the first time Mallory showed up on one of her walks that he was spying on her. She just isn't sure if he is doing it by his own choosing or on Dolion's orders. Regardless, the outcome will be the same.

The walk home is uneventful. Rye and Mallory exchange a few pleasantries, but mostly they walk in silence. Mallory hurries into the depths of the house after helping Rye carry Belamey and the stroller in. There's nobody waiting to question her. In fact, nobody is interested in her at all. The hum of amiable conversation doesn't change in pace or volume. Rye pauses by the front door, feeling the energy of the house. She can't sense anything out of the ordinary and questions her own paranoia.

Chapter 21
Rye Adelgrief

Days turn into weeks, months, and then years.

"Are you breaking some sort of code by allowing me to see you when I can connect you to your bird form and to The Recruiter?" Rye asks Cian the next time he turns up on one of her walks.

"Well, I'm The Recruiter now, and I can make exceptions where I choose." His tone is wistful. Rye's stomach flutters. She doesn't have to look to know that he's gazing at her with his lips parted and discreet desire flaring in his eyes.

Cian has never expressed his feelings for her. A married woman in an impossible position. *Marriage.* Her cheeks colour with shame. She's a married woman, but . . . a headache pulls at the base of her skull. She can feel his emotions in a way that she hasn't been able to with anybody else, and she likes and fears them. Wrinkling her nose, she gives a soft head shake.

She's drawn to Cian in ways she would've never imagined. Right from their first meeting, being with him feels comfortable. There's a voiceless attraction. She's scared to have feelings, scared of how it'll hurt her, scared of what it might mean. Her relationship with Nekane has been strained and turbulent thanks to Dolion and his constant provocation and cynicism. The result is trepidation flowing beneath the surface of Rye's emotions, primal and strong. Almost all her relationships since birth have been marked with a pain that she has no strength to endure. Even her bond with Belamey, her beautiful little boy who toddles on chubby legs, has an undercurrent of pain. A pain her vision says will change their relationship forever.

For three years, she's waited for the vision to come to pass, and the whole time she hoped to avoid it. She tries to make the most of every moment with Belamey. She relives the first time his fat little arms squeezed her neck so often that the ghost of those arms always clings to her. Precious memories. She has worked hard to create those moments. Her hope is that Belamey will carry them too after she's . . .

She pushes the pain and vision away. No point in dwelling on what's coming. She lifts her face to the sun, letting it kiss her cheeks and eyelids, focusing on the hubbub of the children in the playground, laughing and screeching with pleasure. The smell of fresh-cut grass tickles her nose, and all of it combined makes her smile.

"Is that everything you want me to tell Birdie and Pearle?" Cian asks.

Rye opens her eyes and stares at the fluffy clouds cutting a lazy path across the pale blue sky. "Yes, for now. I should return home before someone comes searching for me." She drops her head and peeks at Cian, sheepish. "Thank you for your friendship. I—"

Branches break. A thump and a huff of air cut her off. She stands fast, eyes scanning the trees that line the west wall of the park. Adrenaline surging, she ignores the ruffle of feathers beside her as Cian shifts, climbing to the skies on short wings. There's nothing noticeable in the trees, no movement, and no noise. She strains, trying to see something to explain the knot of negative feelings growing in her.

Cian, having crossed the distance, swoops down under the branches of the trees and disappears into the leaves. She continues watching, knowing Mallory will report to Dolion if he saw her with Cian. Mallory wouldn't know Cian is The Recruiter, but he's still an unknown man that Rye is meeting for unknown reasons. After minutes that feel agonizing, Cian flies toward her. He shifts. "Someone was there. I can't tell who or where they went, concealed by magic."

Rye nods, her panic becoming dread. *Mallory.*

"Perhaps you and Belamey should come with me now. Don't return to the Society of the Blood Wind. I can keep you hidden. Safe."

Rye's lips pull into a tight flat line as she watches Belamey race around the playground, jumping and hooting. His energy makes the smile return to her face. Her hands ball up, and her jaw clenches. "A life in hiding isn't living. I can't do that to him, Cian. I just can't."

The silence lingers. "I'll be watching." He transforms and flies off.

"The tunnels," she calls after him. When he's gone from sight, she collects Belamey and starts the walk to The Society house, a place she has made home since before she was eighteen.

There's no sign of Mallory or anybody else being home. It's an eerie emptiness that's never present. Even Dolion's office is quiet. Rye doesn't discount the idea that they're in the office and they've warded it to keep people from listening in on their conversation.

She chooses not to open the door to check. Bringing the fight to Dolion and whoever might be inside without preparing won't end well. Rye believes she'll have a bit of time before they figure out what needs to be done about her and her sneaking around. So, she was talking to someone in the park? So what? But even as she thinks it, she knows she's kidding herself. She's given Dolion proof that she's not trustworthy, even if it is as simple as meeting a friend they don't know. Her omission of this meeting—maybe they know about the other times—is enough to cast doubt. *Did Mallory hear the conversation between her and Cian? How much do they know or suspect?*

Her time is limited.

Rye has the urge to be still, to let the strange sense of relief sink in; her wait is over. No time. Trembling, she makes her way through the house making deliberate exhales and drawing deep breaths through her nose.

Once Belamey has settled for his nap, she lingers, committing the details of his sweet face in her mind, then she slips into the tunnels. She could leave without letting this come to a head with Nekane, but she knows from her vision that the two of them need to make their peace. Part of her hopes he'll choose a different life.

Wandering in the silence clears her mind. It offers her a refuge, a place that feels like her own, somewhere she doesn't need to hide. In three years, she's never seen or heard any other person in the tunnels. It's become a safe place for her. Her comfort there is so high that she even wears her true appearance.

She heads into the right tunnel today, having travelled it once before. She allows the walls, floors, and roof to be her focal point. The possibility of secret entrances and hidden tunnels is real. When the tunnel forks, she goes left to avoid the dead end but realizes part way into her investigation that she needs to get back before Belamey wakes from his nap. The stumbling of feet and kicked stones echo in the tunnels. A soft murmur of voices reaches her, and she freezes, her blood running cold. She reassumes the appearance that everyone knows her as. Protecting her true identity is a habit.

Creeping toward the lip of her tunnel, she amplifies her vision and hearing. Mallory is picking his way down the other fork in the tunnel, taking deliberate steps to avoid tripping again. There are five small creatures with grey-tattered wings trailing him. Anybody that didn't know would think they were bugs. Rye knows these half-inch tall life forms have humanish faces lacking ears, lips, and hair. They're the living embodiment of curses, another of the things that humans explain away as bad luck. *So, he is cursed. But why are there so many? Usually, one curse torments a Spellbinder.* She watches as they spin in the air, their behaviours energizing. Evil little things, adept at inflicting suffering, maltreatment, and sometimes death.

Mallory swats at one that gets close to his head, yelps, and brushes the wall, almost falling. Five of them can't be a good sign. Rye isn't sure when her body started to shake, she wants to flee but doesn't trust herself to move without creating a disruption. She sees a tiny mouthful of pointed teeth bite down on the side of Mallory's neck. He shrieks and flattens against the wall, bashing at his neck with his hand. Pushing off the wall, he runs in the direction of the dead end. He's swinging his arms over his head.

Rye retracts her vision and slams her eyes shut. Her hearing, amplified, resounds with feet and muffled voices. She crouches and pushes in close to the wall. Her knives are in her hands, coated with magic.

"This is far enough," Dolion says.

Dolion?

There's no response, but their progress stops. Another voice blends with Dolion's. There's no mistaking Nekane's voice. They're chanting, but their words aren't decipherable. The groan of the tunnel and the dark notes of their voices mark their intent. Within seconds, the groan becomes a rumble and crash as the walls and roof collapse, locking Mallory on the other side with five hungry curses.

Abandoning her knives, Rye crouches, curling around herself as a wave of dust gushes down her tunnel. She's still balanced on her feet and rolled tight when she hears Dolion speak. "Mallory served his purpose, fleshing out Rye's true colours. She dies next."

Nekane's silence is heavy as Rye hears their feet move away. Her mouth is dry. She slumps to the ground, eyes closed, as tears leak out of the corners. She stays that way until the cold from the ground creeps into her bones and makes a home. Mallory's cries behind the wall don't last long, pained and frenzied, but he dies fast. Dolion and Nekane sacrificed Mallory to the curses, which can only mean they are breeding them. The curses will eat parts of Mallory and use other parts of his body to lay eggs. If the curses can't get out from behind the collapsed wall, and when Mallory's body is reduced to bones, the curses will continue to eat and lay eggs using each other as food and hosts. *Easy disposal of the man as a problem, and the solution to another? Why reproduce those foul creatures?*

She knows she should flee and not return to the house, but she can't go without Belamey. She hurries for the ladder, terrified he won't be there when she gets home, but as she breaches the hole behind the chair, she hears his sweet voice chattering away to Nekane as they walk into her room. Her tears well up.

She pops out and rushes into the room behind them on wobbly legs.

"Momma," Belamey says, racing into her arms when she bends down. She stares at Nekane over Belamey's head and chokes on her air.

Nekane's posture is stiff, his lips are curled back, and his eyes are wide and fixed on her.

"I go to baseball with Father. I go to hotel after!" Belamey is vibrating with excitement, his voice sing-song.

"Just me and the boy, Rye. You need a night for," he pauses, struggling, "yourself."

So, he doesn't plan to kill me himself. Rye stands motionless, cuddling Belamey to her. He's stopped squirming and nestled his head into her neck as she sways side to side. Her eyes never move from Nekane. Whatever they know, or think they know, they've used it to make their decision. She swallows, moving her tongue in her mouth to create moisture. She parts her lips to speak but closes them without forming words.

Nekane's voice is low, but there's a shake to it that hints at his internal war. He picks his words with care as he tries not to betray his own emotions as well as keep from alarming their son. "If you put him down and hurry, you may continue to breathe another night." A few steps separate Rye and Nekane, but the gulf between them is growing by miles. "Don't try to leave with Belamey. You won't make it out of this room." The conviction in that sentence stabs her.

Her breaths are loud and shallow as she kisses the top of Belamey's head. "Have fun with Father," she says so Nekane can hear. "Momma loves you forever, and even though you may not see me, I'll always be close by," she whispers in Belamey's ear.

He giggles in response to the tickle of her breath. "I see you tomorrow, Momma."

She kisses his round cheek. Her eyes are burning with the tears she's trying to keep him from seeing. He plants a big slobbery kiss on her cheek, and she sets him on the floor. From her crouch, she raises her eyes to Nekane. "I'm sorry, my love," she chokes.

Nekane's expression softens. "You'll have minutes once Belamey and I leave the house." She notes the glistening in his eyes as he scoops up Belamey, but when he stands, his veil of anger is firmly set in place. He marches out, closing the door behind him. The click of it latching makes her jump.

Rye wastes no time catching her voice in a bubble.

She keeps the bubble size minuscule, hoping it will go undetected, and she throws the bubble out of the open window. She captured one word inside: "Help!" *Cian will intercept it,* her brain mutters. Cian insisted on setting an escape plan together the first time she refused to leave Nekane.

Her magnified hearing alerts her to approaching feet on the stairs. She bolts into the hall, scurries behind the chair, and down to the tunnels. Running full speed, her vision is blurred from the tears she's no longer trying to control. The lure of the sparkling tunnel can't penetrate her grief. The only danger they present is if she stumbles blindly into them.

How she climbs the ladder to exit the tunnels is a void in her memory. So much seems to drain away in the moments of her plight. She falls over the edge of the well letting her body tumble onto the ground, oblivious to her surroundings.

Her hands clutch her head as she rocks on her knees with her chin quivering and pressed against her chest. Her shoulders are shaking with repressed sobs; her tear ducts empty of moisture. She's begging for forgiveness, pleading with the image of Belamey to forgive her and love her forever.

Her anguish is making her delirious. She's so lost to herself that she doesn't notice Cian closing the well that she just exited, and she doesn't feel the soft trickle of magic that he sends into her body. The calming effect leads to exhaustion, and within minutes, she's in a coma-like state.

Chapter 22
Rye Adelgrief

When Rye wakes, she lies unmoving, eyes studying the off-white ceiling. She knows by the woodsy, sweet-spicy, and creamy scent in the air that she's with Cian. Part of his ability to calm her body and mind comes from the aroma of sandalwood that clings to him. She senses that he's close, but he gives her the time she needs to compose herself.

She battles the cognitive fog, working to push through the numbness. Her physical and mental movement lack strength. She slides into a sitting position and surveys their sparse surroundings. Cian is sitting with the legs of his chair tipped so it's braced on the wall. He's sipping from a large brown mug and watching her. "Coffee?" His husky voice fills the room.

Refusing to become a victim to her desire to never move again, Rye nods, swinging her feet over the side of the bed. "Where are we?"

"Close to Lindsay. I knew you wouldn't want to go far." He passes her a coffee, which she holds like a lifeline cupped between her hands. The heat from the mug sinks into the flesh of her palms. She lifts it toward her face, feeling the steamy warmth create damp patches on her face where it kisses her skin. Her first sip burns her tongue and leaves a bitter taste in its wake.

She attempts a smile but gives up, knowing it resembles a snarl. She pushes back on the mattress so that she can lean against the wall. "Are they searching for me?"

"They called the police when you disappeared. It's been suggested that you might have run off, but those who know you recognize that you wouldn't leave Belamey. There's a rumour that you were murdered."

"So, I'm missing or murdered? Okay, but are The Society of the Blood Wind looking for me?"

"Not very hard. They have Belamey under constant surveillance, but otherwise, they aren't making any efforts."

Rye stares down into her coffee. The only time she lifts her head is when she sips it, but she does so with her eyes closed. Cian remains silent. When her cup is empty, she sighs and assesses him. "Do you have a plan?"

He nods. "But to do this it means that you and I

become partners, and you, as a vizard, have to remain hidden by personas."

Rye isn't surprised that Cian is aware of her ability to manipulate her appearance. He's The Recruiter, after all, and part of the role is knowing things others wouldn't. Unlike his mentor, Cian can't magically alter his appearance, but that isn't a surprise since it's a rare talent. Cian has been on the fringe of her life, watching for so long. There probably isn't much about her that he doesn't know. "Regular disguises?"

"One for each facet of your life. Our first task is to create a persona that you can wear when you're with Birdie and Pearle—"

"Birdie and Pearle? Why do I need to hide from them?"

"You must hide from everyone if you want to stay alive. Although it appears The Society of the Blood Wind isn't looking for you, they'll stop at nothing to kill you if they learn where you are. You pose a threat to The Society of the Blood Wind because you know so much and because you did what nobody else could do, Rye. You showed they have a weakness."

Rye studies her lap where her hands are twisting and twirling around themselves. "Belamey?"

"He's as good as can be expected under the circumstances."

She looks up, her eyes tearing. "I need to see him?"

Cian says nothing, but he raises his eyebrows in response.

"I can go in just once as Cayen—"

"Be careful with that, Rye."

"Why?"

"When was the last time you saw her?"

Rye scrunches her face. "I can't say for sure. But I saw baby Kieran and baby Kyson and they've been in the house the last two years."

"So?"

"So, if her twins are there, Cayenne has to be."

Cian nods. "Really? Let me check a couple of things before you put this plan into motion. I'll go right now."

Rye stands. If Cian has doubts about Cayenne's whereabouts, then something from his life as The Recruiter is driving those suspicions. Rye trusts him. "Thank you, Cian. It seems inadequate, but I'm not sure what else . . . how else . . . ."

Cian places a hand on her shoulder. His eyes hold hers. "Anything for you, Rye. You know that." The underlying confession of his feelings is unquestionable.

She holds his eyes. "Cian, I may never love again."

"I accept that, Rye, as I always have." He shifts. The movement of his wings wafts his exotic fragrance into her face, causing her mind to settle and the tension to drain from her body. She watches the open window for a while after he's gone.

To pass the time, she changes herself into Cayenne and back to herself a few times. Cayenne gave birth to the twins a year after Belamey was born. Rye knows little about it because Cayenne never forgave her for that day in Dolion's office. Cayenne's behaviour became increasingly more erratic and high risk, so Rye steered clear. Even after the twins were born, there was no contact between them. The twins could be heard crying, but the only time they were seen was when one of the hired helpers was tending to them.

Rye shakes her head, tired of thinking about Cayenne. She focuses on creating the persona she'll use when she interacts with Birdie and Pearle. The efforts exhaust her in her emotionally charged state, and she falls asleep.

The smell of coffee wakes her. She slept the night through. She doesn't roll over when she talks. "And?"

Cian waits in silence for her to reposition before passing her a carrot muffin and a coffee. Rye assesses him. His bulky muscles are strained and his short, thick neck is stiff.

"What?"

"Cayenne is dead."

The moisture in Rye's mouth is gone and the bite of muffin feels grainy and heavy. *Dead!* She spits it out into a napkin and bolts to the bathroom, making it to the toilet before her stomach retches out its limited contents. She sits on the floor, trying to steady her shaking. When she's confident that she can control her body, she returns to her seat on the bed. Cian hands her coffee to her. She sucks a deep gulp, swishing the hot liquid in her mouth.

Her voice is shaky. "Okay, start at the beginning please, Cian."

"She's dead, and the nanny is the primary caregiver to her twin boys and Belamey."

"Did they . . . did they kill her?"

"Probably, but there's no evidence to prove it. She's been dead a while, Rye. You need to consider the implication of that. You lived in that house and didn't know."

Rye has no eagerness to think about that at all. "The boys' father?"

Cian shrugs. "Dead, hiding, unknown. Best guess."

"Okay, well, I'm still going in. I have to see Belamey." In a puff of blue feathers, she soars out the window. She doesn't wait to see if Cian will have objections.

She morphs into a stranger and walks past The Society House just as Lori Cleo walks out. Minutes later, Rye is marching up the steps, adjusting her oversized breasts and chomping on gum so hard that her jaw aches. She walks right in wearing Lori as her own skin; reaching Belamey's room is Rye's goal. The house is just as she remembers it. She attempts to run a hand through her frizzy hair, but her fingers just get caught in the tangles. She tries not to draw any comparison between Lori's hair and her own feelings: wild, messy, and unruly. Giving up trying to tame either, she pauses at the top of the stairs.

The three boys are in the hall. Kieran and Kyson, identical twins, are hitting and biting each other. Belamey is standing at a distance, watching them. His little arms are crossed over his chest, his lips pull tight, and he's shaking his head. Rye's breath catches and her heart aches at the sight of him. Before she can do anything about the situation, a hand grabs her neck and squeezes hard.

"I told you to get out of this house, Lori," Nekane hisses.

Rye decides this isn't a fight she wants to pick, not in front of Belamey. So, she allows Nekane to lead her down the stairs toward the front entrance. As they near the door, she pushes Lori's voice out of her voice box. "I don't understand. Why?" Nekane opens the door and shoves her out. She straightens and turns, giving Nekane Lori's glare.

"Those boys are mine now, Lori. I'll raise them as I see fit. Belamey has too much of his mother in him, and those other boys are rough and tough." There's a fondness in his voice when he refers to Kieran and Kyson. "Belamey will toughen up, and you, of all people, have no stake in his welfare." The door slamming shut pushes Lori backwards when it contacts her oversized breasts.

The gum tumbles out of Rye's mouth on the porch as she stands there gaping at the closed door. *Lori is concerned about Belamey?* If Lori is concerned, others will be too. Belamey will be okay. But Nekane, why the newfangled interest in those wild little boys? A high-pitched *kik-kik-kik* call startles Rye. *Cian.* Rye, as Lori, marches off the porch and hurries up the street before she risks shifting and flying away.

Chapter 23
Astrid Sapphirus

Rye zooms in through the window of Cian's apartment behind him and shifts; her mouth moves before either of them settles on their human feet. Her muscles tighten. "Take me to Pearle and Birdie now. I need to test myself." She sets her jaw and presses her lips together, watching Cian. He returns her stare.

She shifts and flies out the window, leaving him no choice but to follow. When the porch of the safe house comes into view, Rye transforms, landing on the banister in her cat-like pose. She's kept her height and weight similar to her physic as Rye, but she's given herself a more youthful appearance. Her eyes are a light brown, she's lightened her complexion, and given herself long thin lips. Her hair is short and spikey with blue-grey streaks in it.

Cian takes the change in her appearance in stride and strolls past her into the sunroom. Rye trails, mentally running through the ways this could go wrong. The only tell that she's apprehensive is a fast lick of her lips to wet them.

The surprised faces of Birdie, Pearle, and Mouz greet Cian and Rye. Cian takes charge of the room, which gives Rye a chance to catch her breath. "I needed to stop in, Birdie, because I have to go out of town on business. This is Astrid Sapphirus." Cian steps to the side. "She's my recruit."

Rye notes her new name, pulling it around her with the movement of her black cloak. She inclines her head to everyone but says nothing, not yet trusting herself to alter her voice. Her belly is a knot of relief at not having her façade caught. But she regrets that she has to hide from these three people in the first place.

"She's a loner, but it's an attribute that makes her an excellent spy and she's a great warrior. So, should you need anything while I'm away, this bird," Cian gives a soft whistle and a messenger bird from within the room flies to him and he whispers to it. "This bird will always know how to find her." The bird cocks its head at Astrid and flies up into the foliage.

"Hello, Astrid," Pearle says and the others echo her.

Astrid allows a soft smile that crinkles the corner of her eyes.

Birdie gives a hoot and claps her hands together. "Time for coffee." Her voice lowers. "We need to discuss

Rye."

Mouz gives a hiss. "That's my cue. I've some hunting and catching to do." His voice is pained.

Astrid's voice surprises everyone. "I've some of my own to do. Mouz, can I join you? I assume you're heading to The Society of the Blood Wind house."

"Loner, eh?" Pearle says, peering at Astrid.

"Cats are loners by trade," Astrid says.

Cian picks up on her blunder. "As my recruit, I made her privy to information that normally I wouldn't share."

Birdie hops into the kitchen, clucking. Pearle moves her eyes between Cian and Astrid with open sparks of doubt. Because of her respect for The Recruiter and his duties, she doesn't ask questions.

Mouz gives Astrid a once-over, nods, transforms and races out the door. Astrid swallows and saunters out the porch door before shifting.

Late in the night, Rye returns to the room she shares with Cian. It's in darkness, and she knows without looking that he hasn't returned. He was telling the truth about having a mission. Rye maintains her persona as Astrid. It's a safer choice. Astrid will be her regular form unless she's alone with Cian. He's the solitary person who knows who she really is. She pushes away the tumult of emotions that threatens her.

She flops down on the bed, thinking about all the times she's held a disguise. Holding it while in the presence of people she cares about, deceiving them, even if it's for her and their safety, is harder than she ever imagined. She held it though with that one minor indiscretion, an error she won't repeat.

Rye's body feels weighed down. Her energy falls away as she thinks about remaining hidden from the people she loves. Meeting Pearle, Birdie, and Mouz was an excellent test run for her other plans, though. Now she knows she can trust herself to be a part of Belamey's life and come and go from The Society of the Blood Wind house wearing an identity without faltering in the face of the pressure. The heaviness of her limbs relaxes a bit with the realization and a warmness spreads through her chest and colours her cheeks at the thought of Belamey.

After what happened when she entered The Society House as Lori, Rye knows she can't go back wearing that skin. But if not Lori, who? Slinking around The Society House with Mouz offered her the solution she needed. An overheard conversation about a new nanny who'll start working the morning shifts, Monday through Saturday, with Sundays off.

Rye's plan is simple. A few days of reconnaissance on the new Spellbinder nanny, Avery Bay, and then a visit to Avery wearing Nekane as a disguise. Rye, as

Nekane, will change Avery's schedule so Rye can fill in and have time with Belamey, even if it'll include the twins.

Exhausted, Rye drifts to sleep and doesn't wake until the glare of the sun beats down on her. "Shit, I slept in." Rye shifts and flies toward The Society House with fast wing strokes, hoping to get there before noon, when Avery's shift ends. Rye is perched on a tree branch when a tall, slender girl in her twenties rushes out the door with a school bag. *Avery Bay.*

Rye spends the next few weeks learning what she can about Avery, a girl with a sweet smile and pleasant disposition. Avery lives simply, balancing classes, homework, and her job. She doesn't have a lot of friends, not because she isn't likeable, but because her spare time is limited. The friends she does have share similar values. There's no significant other in Avery's life, again by choice. Rye doesn't learn much about Avery's parents other than Avery was raised by a single mother who doesn't live close to Lindsay.

When Rye approaches Avery as Nekane, she picks the doorstep of The Society house as the location. Rye waits for the girl to exit on a Saturday afternoon. Risky, but it gives a day in between stints for Avery's mind to reconcile with her new work schedule. Rye would like to take on more than two of Avery's shifts, but her conscience won't let her take that much income from a student. The girl's blue eyes study her through fancy glasses. "We no longer need you to work Tuesday or Thursday mornings, Avery."

Avery's voice is soft. "Okay, Mr. Adelgrief." If Avery was thinking of questioning the change, she hid it well.

Nekane dismisses Avery with a flick of the hand. Rye holds her disguise, waiting for Avery to disappear from sight before marching off the step. Rye turns the corner of the house where she ducks into the trees, shifts into bird form, and flies away.

Chapter 24
Miss Avery

Rye glides into The Society house at six in the morning on Tuesday. She's swiping at the wispy shoulder-length blonde hair and wondering how Avery stands it clinging to the sides of her face.

"Miss Avery," a sweet, familiar voice calls out.

Rye, as Miss Avery, drops to her knees and embraces Belamey as he launches at her. She scoops him up and spins with him. Belamey giggles and clings to her neck. "Did you climb out of your crib, Bel?" Rye gives herself an invisible pat on the back for overhearing Avery referring to him as Bel. Using his full name, when Avery never does, would create confusion.

Belamey stops giggling. "I a big boy, Miss Avery. I sleep in bed, no crib."

Avery kisses the top of Belamey's head. "You sure are a big boy, Bel. Sleeping in a bed at three." She ruffles his dark hair. "Let's go check on your cousins."

Avery can hear Kieran and Kyson before she enters their bedroom. The malodour of soiled diapers is thick in the air. The stink is so powerful that Avery's nose crinkles and she's scrubbing her hands together like she's dry washing them. When she lays her eyes on the twins, they're biting each other and drawing blood. The twins, one year younger than Belamey, are like wild animals. They aren't fighting. They seem to be enjoying both the feeling of sinking their teeth into each other's flesh as well as the discomfort it causes one another. The possibility that they're enjoying the iron taste of each other's blood isn't lost on Avery.

She flicks her fingers at them, blowing them apart with a small puff of air. They fix their attention on her. Nothing they do suggests they're two-year-old children. *Okay, so Avery must not respond to their fighting that way.* Kyson's face turns red and is locked in a sneer, his fists clenched at his sides, but he remains calculated and in control of himself. Avery can see the wheels turning out a plan to retaliate. Kieran, on the other hand, stands and wobbles toward her, swinging his little arms, intent on hitting her.

"Not a chance, mister," Avery says. She pins his arms down with magic and picks him up, mindful of the teeth he's showing her. She kisses him on his cheek and blows puffs of air into the side of his neck. Kieran doesn't laugh or smile. His small body arches away and he starts to shriek.

Avery gives a subtle shake of her head and puts Kieran on the floor. "No hitting, Kieran. And no biting, boys," she says, hating that her faint voice—Avery's voice—has no note of authority.

Belamey and the twins don't play together. Belamey keeps a distance, does his own thing, but watches. Even at this young age, his displeasure with his cousins is evident. It's also apparent that Belamey has already bonded with Avery. He's eager to please her and loves getting tickles and hugs from her.

Rye maintains her composure. While she's in her role as Miss Avery, her pain and discomfort almost disappear and she feels like she could do anything. On the nights when Cian is home, Rye hurries to share Miss Avery's daily experiences with him. He listens to her ramble on as if what she's sharing is the most ground-breaking news of the day. As the connection between Cian and Rye deepens, she's aware that she feels happy being close to him and that she worries about him when he's off on a mission. She's cognizant of how he makes her feel safe and whole.

Nothing about Rye's life is ideal, but she's accepted the flow of it. She spends the next four years pretending to be Avery twice a week. In between, she works for The Recruiter as Astrid or one of the other regular personas that she's created: Lark Rey the magical artifact collector, Eira Sage the security detail who ensures secure transport to clients seeking refuge at safe houses, and Citrine Rose who is a justice seeker that acts as a hitman or as an escort to Allurist Detention Centre.

Rye lives as someone else so often that she struggles to recall who she really is. Always perceptive, Cian calls her back to herself and to him when he can, carving out moments and places of safety where Rye can just be Rye. Without that, without him, she would disappear.

When Rye discovers that Avery has finished her education and gained employment as a teacher at a school out of town, she wears Nekane's skin and fires Avery before Avery has an opportunity to quit. Nobody within The Society of the Blood Wind will keep in contact with someone as mousy as Avery, someone who isn't a Society member. Now Rye is free to act as the nanny every time Avery's services are needed. By this time, Belamey is seven, and Avery's lone responsibility is to feed the boys breakfast and get them to class, with the exception of Saturdays and days off school. Rye assumes the role of Avery for another six years. She savours every moment she can with Belamey, grateful to be a part of his life even if it isn't as his mother.

The twins live in their own world of fighting and

torture. Dolion and Nekane support it and they instruct Avery to interact with the twins only if there's concern that their actions will lead to death. That interaction comes too often. Dolion and Nekane try to force Belamey to hang out with the twins, but he can't be bothered. "Uncivilized" is the word Belamey uses for them. Instead, he searches for Avery, preferring the company of someone who can carry a conversation without looking for an opening to stick a knife in his person.

Time speeds by, and soon Belamey is thirteen and the twins twelve. Nannies are no longer needed and Rye, as Miss Avery, is dismissed by Nekane. Seeing Belamey after that becomes something more like a stolen moment. So, to keep from feeling directionless and lost, Rye throws herself into work, mostly as Astrid, but a few of her other disguises remain active, too. Staying busy is the only way to keep herself from being overwhelmed by her sadness.

Rye knows that Cian has contacted Belamey, an action done to ease Rye's fears for Belamey's safety. Belamey becomes friends with Cian, a father figure in ways that Nekane could never be: supportive and accepting, allowing trust to build. For Belamey's safety, it's a covert relationship. What neither Rye nor Cian expected was for Belamey to want to be employed by The Recruiter. What The Recruiter offers and what he stands for appeal to Belamey. It calls to him, and in his twenties, when he learns that Cian is The Recruiter, Belamey starts to work for him.

After that, Astrid and Belamey become an effective work team, Cian's favourite work team. Rye is once again able to spend time with a son who thinks his mother is dead. The relationship between Astrid and Belamey isn't motherly. Astrid is terrified of what that would do to her. But it's built on respect and like-minded principles.

As the years progress, Astrid becomes the dominant way that Rye defines herself and Belamey—friends and co-workers—never as Rye, as mother and son. She convinces herself so thoroughly of her relationship with Belamey as a friend and co-worker that Cian is almost fooled by it.

That foundation is shaken to the core when after thirteen years of living this way, the War of Magic and the emergence of the Ember stone change it all.

The sky deepens into night as Astrid swoops toward the safe house, bearing news of Kori Ember's family. Astrid shifts out of bird form mid-air and lands in a cat-like pose on the porch banister, and she pulls her thin lips into a smile at the cassowaries. The tall, muscular birds with shaggy black backs and bright blue heads stop. Their focus on Astrid is intense. She knows these birds are Dugal and Hellzel Grogda, twins brought to

Birdie's haven to provide protection, likely a deadly kind. Lethal protection, it's a measure of the magical war and the dangers of protecting the Ember stone. Dugal and Hellzel, the Spellbinders, are best known for their failing grip on reality; Dugal and Hellzel, as cassowaries, are known for fatal jump attacks with the five-inch-long dagger-like claws on their feet. Astrid knows she's on the approved entry list and hopes the Grogda siblings know it, too.

Astrid's muscles are tight under her cloak. She knows Kori and anyone else watching will assume that it's because she's assessing the cassowaries. A tremble occurs in her brain as her eyesight blurs with an oncoming vision. The shaky depiction of Belamey and herself reunited as mother and son is overlaid with Kori's shadow and three rings. Astrid feels her heart freeze with the revelation, and then it begins to pound. It's a brief vision that would have left her wide-eyed and slack-mouthed if she wasn't a master of her emotions and responses. With wonder, she mentally considers Kori. *Who is this girl, and how will she be able to do what I haven't been able to all these years?*

Coming in 2024, the concluding book in The Ember Files.

Book Three

Fin bursts into the living room, hollering my name. A chemical scent similar to nail polish remover wafts into the room with her. Grama Pearle stops with her coffee mug touching her bottom lip, her mouth quivering with a smile. "It must be time for the unveiling," Grama Pearle whispers.

Fin calls me again. Her voice is bubbly with excitement. Her electric green eyes are as round as saucers and her normally well-kept shaggy black bob looks like she was teasing it backwards with a comb. She's so thoroughly covered in splotches of acrylic paint that I wouldn't be surprised if she was naked, wearing painted-on clothing. In fact, even if she didn't look like a madwoman, Fin wearing paint as clothes wouldn't surprise me.

"Have you slept, Fin? Not to mention fed or watered yourself?" I ask with my eyebrows nestled in my hairline.

She takes a second to focus on me and I feel sure that my nut job friend hasn't slept. My life's motto pops into my head as I watch her. When crazy calls, Kori Ember answers. It's not as sexy as my best friend and roommate, Finley Salinger's motto. More commonly known as Fin, her motto is dark stallions, sparking unicorns, and insatiable appetites. But, for me, answering the summons for things unhinged is my encumbrance. With tortoise-like speed, I accepted it. Now I live in an apartment above Just Flavours, a small restaurant owned by Belamey Adelgrief and Fin. Belamey, as is always the case when I think of him, my nerve endings stir and tingle with yearning.

Fin's voice pulls me from the Belamey spiral my brain was about to plummet into. "Kori," she groans like I'm raining on her parade. She's holding a thirty-five by thirty-five-inch canvas behind her. "After days of being locked in my room, I've created the symbol for us, The Influencers." Her smile stretches across her face. "We can hang it in Just Flavours, wink, wink."

Acknowledgements

It takes a team to write and polish a book; I am grateful to all of you.

To my alpha readers, thank you for reading the raw manuscript and for offering valuable insights. Tabitha Cochrane-Avery, you and I have a history that dates back to grade six—always one of my first readers, from school assignments to creative writing. Working together on this manuscript brought back happy memories. My writing process would not be complete without you. And Chrissy Drouin, your excitement and enthusiastic responses to this manuscript and the characters were invigorating and encouraged me when I needed it the most. I cannot thank you enough.

Thank you to my editor, Laura, for all the guidance in making improvements to *Vizard*.

I am grateful to my husband and sons for their continuous support.

Book Club Reading Guide

1. After reading the book, did your expectations change about it?
2. If this book was a movie, series, or play, would you watch it? Would you watch it first and then read it?
3. Did this book evoke a new feeling of empathy for other people and their personal challenges?
4. Is there a quote from the book that stayed with you? What is it and why?
5. Is there a line from the book that you found unsettling or cringe-worthy?
6. Have you read other books by this author? If so, how does this book compare?
7. Do you agree with the decisions made by the main character or other characters?
8. Were there any plot twists? Were they predictable or did they take you by surprise?
9. Do you agree with the ending?
10. Does this book have a hidden message or lesson? What was the author's goal for writing it?